Praise for **Nathan Englander**'s

For the Relief of Unbearable Urges

"Pitch-perfect. . . . [Englander's] wit has glimpses of Philip Roth and Saul Bellow; its subtlety recalls James Joyce's *Dubliners.*" —*Newsweek*

"Provokes an array of reactions, from shocked tears to guilty belly laughs. . . . Nathan Englander has constructed a deeply affecting treatise on the caprices of fate and the inevitability of laughter." —*The Wall Street Journal*

"One of the classiest, most assured, impressive literary debuts I've come across in ten years of reviewing books. . . . The many voices . . . [Englander] has given life to in this collection earn this gifted writer a distinct and distinguished niche of his own."

—Susan Miron, *The Philadelphia Inquirer*

"Extraordinary, insightful writing. Englander is a fresh, awe-inspiring voice." —*San Francisco Chronicle*

"In [Englander's] sharply etched stories, his characters burst their bounds of culture, history and identity." —*USA Today*

"Impressive. . . . A fresh and promising collection, Nathan Englander's rocket is launched."
—*The Washington Post Book World*

"This debut collection reflects a mastery of the short story form. . . . [These stories are] as faceted and polished as gemstones." —*San Diego Union Tribune*

Nathan Englander

For the Relief of Unbearable Urges

Nathan Englander grew up in New York and lives in
Jerusalem. He is a graduate of the Iowa Writers' Workshop
and a recent recipient of the Pushcart Prize. His stories
have appeared in *Story* magazine and *The New Yorker.*

INTERNATIONAL

For the Relief
of
Unbearable
Urges

Elise,

I. a world full of books about harrowing losses and death, this book stands out as something a little lighter and humourous.

lots of love now and forever,

Mark xx

April 24/00.

For the Relief

of

Unbearable

Urges

Nathan Englander

VINTAGE INTERNATIONAL
Vintage Books
A Division of Random House, Inc.
New York

FIRST VINTAGE INTERNATIONAL EDITION, APRIL 2000

Copyright © 1999 by Nathan Englander

Some of the stories in this collection were originally published as follows:
"The Tumblers" in *American Short Fiction* (Fall 1998, no. 31);
"The Gilgul of Park Avenue" in *Atlantic* (March 1999); "The Last One Way" in
The New Yorker (January 18, 1999); "For the Relief of Unbearable Urges,"
"Reb Kringle," and "The Twenty-seventh Man" in *Story* (Spring 1996,
Winter 1997, and Winter 1998).

The Library of Congress has cataloged the Knopf edition as follows:
Englander, Nathan.
For the relief of unbearable urges / Nathan Englander. — 1st ed.
p. cm.
ISBN 0-375-40492-9 (alk. paper)
1. Jews—Social life and customs—Fiction. 2. Jews—Persecutions—Fiction.
3. Orthodox Judaism—Fiction. I. Title.
PS3555.N424F67 1999
813'.54—dc21 98-41727
CIP

Vintage ISBN: 0-375-70443-4

www.vintagebooks.com

Printed in the United States of America
10 9 8 7 6 5 4 3 2 1

For Merle N. Englander

There are many people whose friendship and support have been essential to the creation of this book. The author gratefully acknowledges their contribution and would also like to thank Glen Weldon, Deborah Brodie, and Lois Rosenthal of *Story* magazine. Thank you to Jordan Pavlin for her sensitive and insightful comments. And to Nicole Aragi, agent and cherished friend.

Contents

The Twenty-seventh Man

The orders were given from Stalin's country house at Kuntsevo. He relayed them to the agent in charge with no greater emotion than for the killing of kulaks or clergy or the outspoken wives of very dear friends. The accused were to be apprehended the same day, arrive at the prison gates at the same moment, and—with a gasp and simultaneous final breath—be sent off to their damnation in a single rattling burst of gunfire.

It was not an issue of hatred, only one of allegiance. For Stalin knew there could be loyalty to only one nation. What he did not know so well were the authors' names on his list. When presented to him the next morning he signed the warrant anyway, though there were now twenty-seven, and yesterday there had been twenty-six.

No matter, except maybe to the twenty-seventh.

The orders left little room for variation, and none for tardiness. They were to be carried out in secrecy and—the only point that was reiterated—simultaneously. But how were the agents to get the men from Moscow and Gorky, Smolensk and Penza, Shuya and Podolsk, to the prison near the village of X at the very same time?

The agent in charge felt his strength was in leadership and gave up the role of strategist to the inside of his hat. He cut the list into strips and sprinkled them into the freshly blocked crown, mixing carefully so as not to disturb its shape. Most of these writers were in Moscow. The handful who were in their native villages, taking the waters somewhere, or locked in a cabin trying to finish that seminal work would surely receive a stiff cuffing when a pair of agents, aggravated by the trek, stepped through the door.

After the lottery, those agents who had drawn a name warranting a long journey accepted the good-natured insults and mockery of friends. Most would have it easy, nothing more to worry about than hurrying some old rebel to a car, or getting their shirts wrinkled in a heel-dragging, hair-pulling rural scene that could be as messy as necessary in front of a pack of superstitious peasants.

Then there were those who had it hard. Such as the two agents assigned to Vasily Korinsky, who, seeing no way out, was prepared to exit his bedroom quietly but whose wife, Paulina, struck the shorter of the two officers with an Oriental-style brass vase. There was a scuffle, Paulina was subdued, the short officer taken out unconscious, and a precious hour lost on their estimated time.

There was the pair assigned to Moishe Bretzky, a true lover of vodka and its country of origin. One would not have pegged him as one of history's most sensitive Yiddish poets. He was huge, slovenly, and smelly as a horse. Once a year, during the Ten Days of Penitence, he would take notice of his sinful ways and sober up for Yom Kippur. After the fast, he would grab pen and pad and write furiously for weeks in his sister's vent-less kitchen—the shroud of atonement still draped over his splitting head. The finished work was toasted with a brimming shot of vodka. Then Bretzky's thirst would begin to rage and off he would go for another year. His sister's husband would have put an end to this annual practice if it weren't for the rubles he received for the sweat-curled pages Bretzky abandoned.

It took the whole of the night for the two agents to locate Bretzky. They tracked him down in one of the whorehouses that did not exist, and if they did, government agents surely did not frequent them. Nonetheless, having escaped notice, they slipped into the room. Bretzky was passed out on his stomach with a smiling trollop pinned under each arm. The time-consuming process of freeing the whores, getting Bretzky upright, and moving him into the hallway reduced the younger man to tears.

The senior agent left his partner in charge of the body while he went to chat with the senior woman of the house. Introducing himself numerous times, as if they had never met, he explained his predicament and enlisted the help of a dozen women.

Twelve of the house's strongest companions—in an array of pink and red robes, froufrou slippers, and painted toenails—carried the giant bear to the waiting car amid a roar of giggles. It was a sight Bretzky would have enjoyed tremendously had he been conscious.

The least troubling of the troublesome abductions was that of Y. Zunser, oldest of the group and a target of the first serious verbal attacks on the cosmopolitans back in '49. In the February 19 edition of *Literaturnaya Gazeta* he had been criticized as an obsolete author, accused of being anti-Soviet, and chided for using a pen name to hide his Jewish roots. In that same edition they printed his real name, Melman, stripping him of the privacy he had so enjoyed.

Three years later they came for him. The two agents were not enthusiastic about the task. They had shared a Jewish literature instructor in high school, whom they admired despite his ethnicity and who even coerced them into writing a poem or two. Both were rather decent fellows, and capturing an eighty-one-year-old man did not exactly jibe with their vision of bravely serving the party. They were simply following instructions. But somewhere amid their justifications lay a deep fear of punishment.

It was not yet dawn and Zunser was already dressed, sitting with a cup of tea. The agents begged him to stand up on his own, one of them trying the name Zunser and the other pleading with Melman. He refused.

"I will neither resist nor help. The responsibility must rest fully upon your conscience."

"We have orders," they said.

"I did not say you were without orders. I said that you have to bear responsibility."

They first tried lifting him by his arms, but Zunser was too delicate for the maneuver. Then one grabbed his ankles while the other clasped his chest. Zunser's head lolled back. The agents were afraid of killing him, an option they had been warned against. They put him on the floor and the larger of the two scooped him up, cradling the old man like a child.

Zunser begged a moment's pause as they passed a portrait of his deceased wife. He fancied the picture had a new moroseness to it, as if the sepia-toned eyes might well up and shed a tear. He spoke aloud. "No matter, Katya. Life ended for me on the day of your death; everything since has been but nostalgia." The agent shifted the weight of the romantic in his arms and headed out the door.

The solitary complicated abduction that took place out of Moscow was the one that should have been the easiest of the twenty-seven. It was the simple task of removing Pinchas Pelovits from the inn on the road that ran to X and the prison beyond.

Pinchas Pelovits had constructed his own world with a compassionate God and a diverse group of worshipers. In it, he tested these people with moral dilemmas and tragedies—

testing them sometimes more with joy and good fortune. He recorded the trials and events of this world in his notebooks in the form of stories and novels, essays, poems, songs, anthems, tales, jokes, and extensive histories that led up to the era in which he dwelled.

His parents never knew what label to give their son, who wrote all day but did not publish, who laughed and cried over his novels but was gratingly logical in his contact with the everyday world. What they did know was that Pinchas wasn't going to take over the inn.

When they became too old to run the business, the only viable option was to sell out at a ridiculously low price— provided the new owners would leave the boy his room and feed him when he was hungry. Even when the business became the property of the state, Pinchas, in the dreamer's room, was left in peace: *Why bother, he's harmless, sort of a good-luck charm for the inn, no one even knows he's here, maybe he's writing a history of the place, and we'll all be made famous.* He wasn't. But who knows, maybe he would have, had his name—mumbled on the lips of travelers—not found its way onto Stalin's list.

The two agents assigned Pinchas arrived at the inn driving a beat-up droshky and posing as the sons of now poor landowners, a touch they thought might tickle their superiors. One carried a Luger (a trinket he brought home from the war), and the other kept a billy club stashed in his boot. They found the narrow hallway with Pinchas's room and knocked lightly on his door. "Not hungry" was the response. The agent with the Luger gave the door a hip check; it didn't budge. "Try the handle," said the voice. The agent did, swinging it open.

"You're coming with us," said the one with the club in his boot.

"Absolutely not," Pinchas stated matter-of-factly. The

agent wondered if his "You're coming with us" had sounded as bold.

"Put the book down on the pile, put your shoes on, and let's go." The agent with the Luger spoke slowly. "You're under arrest for anti-Soviet activity."

Pinchas was baffled by the charge. He meditated for a moment and came to the conclusion that there was only one moral outrage he'd been involved in, though it seemed to him a bit excessive to be incarcerated for it.

"Well, you can have them, but they're not really mine. They were in a copy of a Zunser book that a guest forgot and I didn't know where to return them. Regardless, I studied them thoroughly. You may take me away." He proceeded to hand the agents five postcards. Three were intricate pen-and-ink drawings of a geisha in various positions with her legs spread wide. The other two were identical photographs of a sturdy Russian maiden in front of a painted tropical background wearing a hula skirt and making a vain attempt to cover her breasts. Pinchas began stacking his notebooks while the agents divvied the cards. He was sad that he had not resisted temptation. He would miss taking his walks and also the desk upon whose mottled surface he had written.

"May I bring my desk?"

The agent with the Luger was getting fidgety. "You won't be needing anything, just put on your shoes."

"I'd much prefer my books to shoes," Pinchas said. "In the summer I sometimes take walks without shoes but never without a novel. If you would have a seat while I organize my notes—" and Pinchas fell to the floor, struck in the head with the pistol grip. He was carried from the inn rolled in a blanket, his feet poking forth, bare.

Pinchas awoke, his head throbbing from the blow and the exceedingly tight blindfold. This was aggravated by the sound of ice cracking under the droshky wheels, as happens along the river route west of X. "The bridge is out on this road," he told them. "You'd best cut through the old Bunakov place. Everybody does it in winter."

The billy club was drawn from the agent's boot, and Pinchas was struck on the head once again. The idea of arriving only to have their prisoner blurt out the name of the secret prison was mortifying. In an attempt to confound him, they turned off on a clearly unused road. There are reasons that unused roads are not used. It wasn't half a kilometer before they had broken a wheel and it was off to a nearby pig farm on foot. The agent with the gun commandeered a donkey-drawn cart, leaving a furious pig farmer cursing and kicking the side of his barn.

The trio were all a bit relieved upon arrival: Pinchas because he started to get the idea that this business had to do with something more than his minor infraction, and the agents because three other cars had shown up only minutes before they had—all inexcusably late.

By the time the latecomers had been delivered, the initial terror of the other twenty-three had subsided. The situation was tense and grave, but also unique. An eminent selection of Europe's surviving Yiddish literary community was being held within the confines of an oversized closet. Had they known they were going to die, it might have been different. Since they didn't, I. J. Manger wasn't about to let Mani Zaretsky see him cry for rachmones. He didn't have time to anyway. Pyotr Kolyazin, the famed atheist, had already dragged him into a heated discussion about the ramifications of using God's will to drastically alter the outcome of previously "logical" plots. Manger took this to be an attack on his work and asked Kolyazin if he labeled everything he didn't understand "illogical." There was also the present situation to discuss, as well as old rivalries, new poems, disputed reviews, journals that just aren't the same, up-and-coming editors, and, of course, the gossip, for hadn't they heard that Lev had used his latest manuscript for kindling?

When the noise got too great, a guard opened the peephole in the door to find that a symposium had broken loose. As a result, by the time numbers twenty-four through twenty-seven arrived, the others had already been separated into smaller cells.

Each cell was meant to house four prisoners and contained three rotting mats to sleep on. In a corner was a bucket. There were crude holes in the wood-plank walls, and it was hard to tell if the captors had punched them as a form of ventilation or if the previous prisoners had painstakingly scratched them through to confirm the existence of a world outside.

The four latecomers had lain down immediately, Pinchas on the floor. He was dazed and shivering, stifling his moans so the others might rest. His companions did not even think of sleep: Vasily Korinsky because of worry about what might be the outcome for his wife; Y. Zunser because he was trying to adapt to the change (the only alteration he had planned for in his daily routine was death, and that in his sleep); Bretzky because he hadn't really awakened.

Excepting Pinchas, none had an inkling of how long they'd traveled, whether from morning until night or into the next day. Pinchas tried to use his journey as an anchor, but in the dark he soon lost his notion of time gone by. He listened for the others' breathing, making sure they were alive.

The lightbulb hanging from a frayed wire in the ceiling went on. This was a relief; not only an end to the darkness but a separation, a seam in the seeming endlessness.

They stared unblinking into the dim glow of the bulb and

worried about its abandoning them. All except Bretzky, whose huge form already ached for a vodka and who dared not crack an eye.

Zunser was the first to speak. "With morning there is hope."

"For what?" asked Korinsky out of the side of his mouth. His eye was pressed up against a hole in the back wall.

"A way out," Zunser said. He watched the bulb, wondering how much electricity there was in the wire, how he would reach it, and how many of them it would serve.

Korinsky misunderstood the statement to be an optimistic one. "Feh on your way out and feh on your morning. It's pitch dark outside. Either it's night or we're in a place with no sun. I'm freezing to death."

The others were a bit shocked when Bretzky spoke: "Past the fact that you are not one of the whores I paid for and this is not the bed we fell into, I'm uncertain. Whatever the situation, I shall endure it, but without your whining about being cold in front of an old man in shirtsleeves and this skinny one with no shoes." His powers of observation were already returning and Yom Kippur still months away.

"I'm fine," said Pinchas. "I'd much rather have a book than shoes."

They all knitted their brows and studied the man; even Bretzky propped himself up on an elbow.

Zunser laughed, and then the other three started in. Yes, it would be much better to have a book. Whose book? Surely not the pamphlet by that fool Horiansky—this being a well-publicized and recent failure. They laughed some more. Korinsky stopped, worrying that one of the other men in the room might be Horiansky. Horiansky, thankfully, was on the other end of the hall and was spared that final degradation before his death.

No one said another word until the lightbulb went off again, and then they remained silent because it was supposed to be night. However, it was not. Korinsky could see light seeping through the holes and chinks in the boards. He would tell them so when the bulb came back on, if it did.

Pinchas could have laughed indefinitely, or at least until the time of his execution. His mind was not trained, never taught any restraint or punished for its reckless abandon. He had written because it was all that interested him, aside from his walks, and the pictures at which he had peeked. Not since childhood had he skipped a day of writing.

Composing without pen and paper, he decided on something short, something he could hone, add a little bit to every day until his release.

Zunser felt the coldness of the floor seeping into his bones, turning them brittle. It was time anyway. He had lived a long life, enjoyed recognition for something he loved doing. All the others who had reached his level of fame had gone to the ovens or were in America. How much more meaningless was success with the competition gone? Why write at all when your readers have been turned to ash? Never outlive your language. Zunser rolled onto his side.

Bretzky sweated the alcohol out of his blood. He tried to convince himself that it was a vision of drink, a clearer vision because he was getting older, but a hallucination nonetheless. How many times had he turned, after hearing his name called, to find no one? He fumbled for a breast, a soft pink cheek, a swatch of satin, and fell asleep.

Before closing his eyes only to find more darkness, Pinchas recited the first paragraph a final time:

The morning that Mendel Muskatev awoke to find his desk was gone, his room was gone, and the sun was gone, he assumed he had died. This worried him, so he said the prayer for the dead, keeping himself in mind. Then he wondered if one was allowed to do such a thing, and worried instead that the first thing he had done upon being dead was sin.

When the light came on, Korinsky stirred noticeably, as if to break the ice, as if they were bound by the dictates of civilized society. "You know it isn't morning, it's about nine o'clock or ten, midnight at the latest."

Pinchas was reciting his paragraph quietly, playing with the words, making changes, wishing he had a piece of slate.

Korinsky waited for an answer, staring at the other three. It was hard to believe they were writers. He figured he too must be disheveled, but at least there was some style left in him. These others, a drunk, an incontinent old curmudgeon, and an idiot, could not be of his caliber. Even the deficient Horiansky would be appreciated now. "I said, it's not morning. They're trying to fool us, mess up our internal clocks."

"Then go back to sleep and leave us to be fooled." Bretzky had already warned this sot yesterday. He didn't need murder added to his list of trumped-up charges.

"You shouldn't be so snide with me. I'm only trying to see if we can maintain a little dignity while they're holding us here."

Zunser had set himself up against a wall. He had folded his mat and used it like a chair, cushioning himself from the splinters. "You say 'holding' as if this is temporary and in the next stage we will find ourselves someplace more to our liking."

Korinsky looked at Zunser, surveying him boldly. He did not like being goaded, especially by some old coot who had no idea to whom he was talking.

"Comrade," he addressed Zunser in a most acerbic tone, "I am quite sure my incarceration is due to bureaucratic confusion of some sort. I've no idea what you wrote that landed you here, but I have an impeccable record. I was a principal member of the Anti-Fascist Committee, and my ode, *Stalin of Silver, Stalin of Gold*, happens to be a national favorite."

"'We spilled our blood in revolution, only to choke on Stalin's pollution.'" Bretzky quoted a bastardization of Korinsky's ballad.

"How dare you mock me!"

"I've not had the pleasure of hearing the original," Zunser said, "but I must say the mockery is quite entertaining."

"'Our hearts cheered as one for revolution, now we bask in the glory of great Stalin's solution.'" All three heads turned to Pinchas, Korinsky's the quickest.

"Perfect." Korinsky sneered at the other two men. "I must say it is nice to be in the presence of at least one fan."

Among the many social interactions Pinchas had never before been involved in, this was one. He did not know when adulation was being requested.

"Oh, I'm no fan, sir. You're a master of the Yiddish language, but the core of all your work is flawed by a heavy-handed party message that has nothing to do with the people about whom you write." This with an eloquence which to Korinsky sounded like the fool was condescending.

"The characters are only vehicles, fictions!" He was shouting at Pinchas. Then he caught himself shouting at an idiot, while the other two men convulsed with laughter.

"They are very real," said Pinchas before returning to his rocking and mumbling.

"What are you two fops making fun of? At least I have a body of work that is read."

Bretzky was angry again. "Speak to me as you like. If it begins to bother me too much, I'll pinch your head off from your neck." He made a pinching motion with his massive fingers. "But I must warn you against speaking to your elders with disrespect. Furthermore, I have a most cloudy feeling that the face on the old man also belongs to the legendary Zunser, whose accomplishments far exceed those of any of the writers, Yiddish or otherwise, alive in Russia today."

"Zunser?" said Korinsky.

"Y. Zunser!" screamed Pinchas. He could not imagine being confined with such a singular mind. Pinchas had never even considered that Zunser was an actual person. My God, he had seen the great seer pee into a bucket. "Zunser," he said to the man. He stood and banged his fist against the door, screaming "Zunser" over and over again, like it was a password his keepers would understand and know the game was finished.

A guard came down the hall and beat Pinchas to the floor. He left them a bowl of water and a few crusts of black bread. The three ate quickly. Bretzky held up the casualty while Zunser poured some water into his mouth, made him swallow.

"The man is crazy, he is going to get us all killed." Korinsky sat with his eye against a knothole, peering into the darkness of their day.

"Maybe us, but who would dare to kill the poet laureate of the Communist empire?" Bretzky's tone was biting, though his outward appearance did not reflect it. He cradled Pinchas's limp form while Zunser mopped the boy's brow with his sleeve.

"This is no time for joking. I was going to arrange for a meeting with the warden, but that lunatic's screaming fouled it up. Swooning like a young girl. Has he never before met a man he admired?" Korinsky hooked a finger through one of the larger holes, as if he were trying to feel the texture of the darkness outside. "Who knows when that guard will return?"

"I would not rush to get out," said Zunser. "I can assure you there is only one way to exit."

"Your talk gets us nowhere." Korinsky stood and leaned a shoulder against a cold board.

"And what has gotten you somewhere?" said Zunser. "Your love ballads to the regime? There are no hoofbeats to be heard in the distance. Stalin doesn't spur his horse, racing to your rescue."

"He doesn't know. He wouldn't let them do this to me."

"Maybe not to you, but to the Jew that has your name and lives in your house and lies next to your wife, yes." Zunser massaged a stiffening knee.

"It's not my life. It's my culture, my language. No more."

"Only your language?" Zunser waved him away. "Who are we without Yiddish?"

"The four sons of the Passover seder, at best." Korinsky sounded bitter.

"This is more than tradition, Korinsky. It's blood." Bretzky spat into the pail. "I used to drink with Kapler, shot for shot."

"And?" Korinsky kept his eye to a hole but listened closely.

"And have you seen a movie directed by Kapler lately? He made a friendship with the exalted comrade's daughter. Now he is in a labor camp—if he's alive. Stalin did not take too well to Jewish hands on his daughter's pure white skin."

"You two wizards can turn a Stalin to a Hitler."

Bretzky reached over and gave Korinsky a pat on the leg. "We don't need the Nazis, my friend."

"Feh, you're a paranoid, like all drunks."

Zunser shook his head. He was tiring of the Communist and worried about the boy. "He's got a fever. And he's lucky if there isn't a crack in that head." The old man took off his shoes and put his socks on Pinchas.

"Let me," said Bretzky.

"No," Zunser said. "You give him the shoes, mine won't fit him." Pinchas's feet slipped easily into Bretzky's scuffed and cracking shoes.

"Here, take it." Korinsky gave them his mat. "Believe me, it's not for the mitzvah. I just couldn't stand to spend another second trapped with your righteous stares."

"The eyes you feel are not ours," said Zunser.

Korinsky glowered at his wall.

Pinchas Pelovits was not unconscious. He had only lost his way. He heard the conversations, but paid them little heed. The weight of his body lay on him like a corpse. He worked on his story, saying it aloud to himself, hoping the others would hear and follow it and bring him back.

Mendel figured he'd best consult the local rabbi, who might be able to direct him in such matters. It was Mendel's first time visiting the rabbi in his study—not having previously concerned himself with the nuances of worship. Mendel was much surprised to find that the rabbi's study was of the exact dimensions of his missing room. In fact, it appeared that the tractate the man was poring over rested on the missing desk.

The bulb glowed. And with light came relief. What if they had been left in the darkness? They hated the bulb for its control, such a flimsy thing.

They had left a little water for the morning. Again, Bretzky held Pinchas while Zunser tipped the bowl against the boy's lips. Korinsky watched, wanting to tell them to be careful not to spill, to make sure they saved some for him.

Pinchas sputtered, then said, "Fine, that's fine." He spoke loudly for someone in such apparent ill health. Zunser passed the bowl to Korinsky before taking his own sip.

"Very good to have you with us," said Zunser, trying to catch the boy's eyes with his own. "I wanted to ask you, why is my presence so unsettling? We are all writers here, if I understand the situation correctly."

Zunser used Bretzky to belabor the point. "Come on, tell the boy who you are."

"Moishe Bretzky. They call me The Glutton in the gossip columns."

Zunser smiled at the boy. "You see. A big name. A legend for his poetry, as much for his antics. Now, tell us. Who are you?"

"Pinchas Pelovits."

None had heard the name. Zunser's curiosity was piqued. Bretzky didn't care either way. Korinsky was only further pained at having to put up with a madman who wasn't even famous.

"I am the one who doesn't belong here," Pinchas said. "Though if I could, I'd take the place of any of you."

"But you are not here in place of us, you are here as one of us. Do you write?"

"Oh, yes, that's all I do. That's all I've ever done, except for reading and my walks."

"If it makes any difference, we welcome you as an equal." Zunser surveyed the cubicle. "I'd much rather be saying this to you in my home."

"Are you sure I'm here for being a writer?" Pinchas looked at the three men.

"Not just for being a writer, my friend." Bretzky clapped him lightly on the back. "You are here as a subversive writer. An enemy of the state! Quite a feat for an unknown."

The door opened and all four were dragged from the cell and taken by a guard to private interrogation chambers— Bretzky escorted by three guards of his own. There they were beaten, degraded, made to confess to numerous crimes, and to sign confessions that they had knowingly distributed Zionist propaganda aimed at toppling the Soviet government.

Zunser and Pinchas had been in adjoining chambers and heard each other's screams. Bretzky and Korinsky also shared a common wall, though there was silence after each blow. Korinsky's sense of repute was so strong that he stifled his screaming. Bretzky did not call out. Instead he cried and cried. His abusers mocked him for it, jeering at the overgrown baby. His tears did not fall from the pain, however. They came out of the sober realization of man's cruelty and the picture of the suffering being dealt to his peers, especially Zunser.

Afterward, they were given a fair amount of water, a hunk of bread, and some cold potato-and-radish soup. They were returned to the same cell in the darkness. Zunser and Pinchas needed to be carried.

Pinchas had focused on his story, his screams sounding as if they were coming from afar. With every stripe he received, he added a phrase, the impact reaching his mind like the dull rap of a windowpane settling in its sash:

"Rabbi, have you noticed we are without a sun today?" Mendel asked by way of an introduction.

"My shutters are closed against the noise."

"Did no one else mention it at morning prayers?"

"No one else arrived," said the rabbi, continuing to study.

"Well, don't you think that strange?"

"I had. I had until you told me about this sun. Now I understand—no sensible man would get up to greet a dawn that never came."

They were all awake when the bulb went on. Zunser was making peace with himself, preparing for certain death. The fingers of his left hand were twisted and split. Only his thumb had a nail.

Pinchas had a question for Zunser. "All your work treats fate as if it were a mosquito to be shooed away. All your characters struggle for survival and yet you play the victim. You had to have known they would come."

"You have a point," Zunser said, "a fair question. And I answer it with another: Why should I always be the one to survive? I watched Europe's Jews go up the chimneys. I buried a wife and a child. I do believe one can elude the fates. But why assume the goal is to live?" Zunser slid the mangled hand onto his stomach. "How many more tragedies do I want to survive? Let someone take witness of mine."

Bretzky disagreed. "We've lost our universe, this is true. Still, a man can't condemn himself to death for the sin of living. We can't cower in the shadows of the camps forever."

"I would give anything to escape," said Korinsky.

Zunser turned his gaze toward the bulb. "That is the single rule I have maintained in every story I ever wrote. The desperate are never given the choice."

"Then," asked Pinchas, and to him there was no one else but his mentor in the room, "you don't believe there is any reason I was brought here to be with you? It isn't part of anything larger, some cosmic balance, a great joke of the heavens?"

"I think that somewhere a clerk made a mistake."

"That," Pinchas said, "I cannot bear."

All the talking had strained Zunser and he coughed up a bit of blood. Pinchas attempted to help Zunser but couldn't stand up. Bretzky and Korinsky started to their feet. "Sit, sit," Zunser said. They did, but watched him closely as he tried to clear his lungs.

Pinchas Pelovits spent the rest of that day on the last lines of his story. When the light went out, he had already finished.

They hadn't been in darkness long when they were awakened by the noise and the gleam from the bulb. Korinsky immediately put his eye to the wall.

"They are lining up everyone outside. There are machine guns. It is morning, and everyone is blinking as if they were newly born."

Pinchas interrupted. "I have something I would like to recite. It's a story I wrote while we've been staying here."

"Go ahead," said Zunser.

"Let's hear it," said Bretzky.

Korinsky pulled the hair from his head. "What difference can it make now?"

"For whom?" asked Pinchas, and then proceeded to recite his little tale:

The morning that Mendel Muskatev awoke to find his desk was gone, his room was gone, and the sun was gone, he assumed he had died. This worried him, so he said the prayer for the dead, keeping himself in mind. Then he wondered if one was allowed to do such a thing, and worried instead that the first thing he had done upon being dead was sin.

Mendel figured he'd best consult the local rabbi, who might be able to direct him in such matters. It was Mendel's first time visiting the rabbi in his study—not having previously concerned himself with the nuances of worship. Mendel was much surprised to find that the rabbi's study was of the exact dimensions of his missing room. In fact, it appeared that the tractate the man was poring over rested on the missing desk.

"Rabbi, have you noticed we are without a sun today?" Mendel asked by way of an introduction.

"My shutters are closed against the noise."

"Did no one else mention it at morning prayers?"

"No one else arrived," said the rabbi, continuing to study.

"Well, don't you think that strange?"

"I had. I had until you told me about this sun. Now I understand—no sensible man would get up to greet a dawn that never came."

"This is all very startling, Rabbi. But I think we—at some point in the night—have died."

The rabbi stood up, grinning. "And here I am with an eternity's worth of Talmud to study."

Mendel took in the volumes lining the walls.

"I've a desk and a chair, and a shtender in the corner should I want to stand," said the rabbi. "Yes, it would seem I'm in heaven." He patted Mendel on the shoulder. "I must thank you for rushing over to tell me." The rabbi shook Mendel's hand and nodded good-naturedly, already searching for his place in the text. "Did you come for some other reason?"

"I did," said Mendel, trying to find a space between the books where once there was a door. "I wanted to know"—and here his voice began to quiver—"which one of us is to say the prayer?"

Bretzky stood. "Bravo," he said, clapping his hands. "It's like a shooting star. A tale to be extinguished along with the teller." He stepped forward to meet the agent in charge at the door. "No, the meaning, it was not lost on me."

Korinsky pulled his knees into his chest, hugged them. "No," he admitted, "it was not lost."

Pinchas did not blush or bow his head. He stared at Zunser, wondered what the noble Zunser was thinking, as they were driven from the cell.

Outside all the others were being assembled. There were Horiansky and Lubovitch, Lev and Soltzky. All those great voices with the greatest stories of their lives to tell, and forced to take them to the grave. Pinchas, having increased his readership threefold, had a smile on his face.

Pinchas Pelovits was the twenty-seventh, or the fourteenth from either end, if you wanted to count his place in line. Bretzky supported Pinchas by holding up his right side, for his equilibrium had not returned. Zunser supported him on the left, but was in bad shape himself.

"Did you like it?" Pinchas asked.

"Very much," Zunser said. "You're a talented boy."

Pinchas smiled again, then fell, his head landing on the stockingless calves of Zunser. One of his borrowed shoes flew forward, though his feet slid backward in the dirt. Bretzky fell atop the other two. He was shot five or six times, but being such a big man and such a strong man, he lived long enough to recognize the crack of the guns and know that he was dead.

The Tumblers

Who would have thought that a war of such proportions would bother to turn its fury against the fools of Chelm? Never before, not by smallpox or tax collectors, was the city intruded upon by the troubles of the outside world.

The Wise Men had seen to this when the town council was first founded. They drew up a law on a length of parchment, signed it, stamped on their seal, and nailed it, with much fanfare, to a tree: Not a wind, not a whistle, not the shadow from a cloud floating outside city limits, was welcome in the place called Chelm.

These were simple people with simple beliefs, who simply wanted to be left to themselves. And they were for generations, no one going in and only stories coming out, as good stories somehow always do. Tales of the Wise Men's logic, most notably of Mendel's grandfather, Gronam the Ox, spread, as the war later would, to the far corners of the earth.

In the Fulton Street Fish Market the dockworkers laughed with Yiddish good humor upon hearing how Gronam had tried to drown a carp. At a dairy restaurant in Buenos Aires, a customer was overcome with hiccups as his waiter recounted the events of the great sour cream shortage, explaining how Gronam had declared that water was sour cream and sour cream water, single-handedly saving the Feast of Weeks from complete and total ruin.

How the stories escaped is no great mystery, for though outsiders were unwelcome, every few years someone would pass through. There had been, among the trespassers, one vagrant and one vamp, one troubadour lost in a blizzard and one horse trader on a mule. A gypsy tinker with a friendly face stayed a week. He put new hinges on all the doors while his wife told fortunes to the superstitious in the shade of the square. Of course, the most famous visit of all was made by the circus troupe that planted a tent and put on for three days show after show. Aside from these few that came through the center of town, there was also, always, no matter what some say, a black market thriving on the outskirts of Chelm. For where else did the stores come up with their delicacies? Even the biggest deniers of its existence could be seen eating a banana now and then.

Gronam's logic was still employed when the invaders built the walls around a corner of the city, creating the Ghetto of Chelm. There were so many good things lacking and so many bad in abundance that the people of the ghetto renamed almost all that they had: they called their aches "mother's milk," and darkness became "freedom"; filth they referred to as "hope"—and felt for a while, looking at each other's hands and faces and soot-blackened clothes, fortunate. It was only death that they could not rename, for they had nothing to put in its place. This is when they became sad and felt their hunger and when some began to lose their faith in God. This is when the Mahmir Rebbe, the most pious of them all, sent Mendel outside the walls.

It was no great shock to Mendel, for the streets outside the cramped ghetto were the streets of their town, the homes their homes, even if others now lived in them. The black market was the same except that it had been made that much more clandestine and greedy by the war. Mendel was happy to find that his grandfather's wisdom had been adopted among the peasants with whom he dealt. Potatoes were treated as gold, and a sack of gold might as well have been potatoes. Mendel traded away riches' worth of the latter (now the former) for as much as he could conceal on his person of the former (now the latter). He took the whole business to be a positive sign, thinking that people were beginning to regain their good sense.

The successful transaction gave Mendel a touch of real confidence. Instead of sneaking back the way he came, he ventured past the front of the icehouse and ignored the first signs of a rising sun. He ran through the alley behind Cross-eyed Bilha's store and skirted around the town square, keeping on until he arrived at his house. It was insanity—or suicide—for him to be out there. All anyone would need was a glimpse of him to know, less than that even, their senses had become so sharp. And what of the fate of the potatoes? They surely wouldn't make it to the ghetto if Mendel were caught and strung up from the declaration tree with a sign that said SMUG-GLER hung around his neck. Those precious potatoes that filled his pockets and lined his long underwear from ankles to elbows would all go to waste, softening up and sprouting eyes. But Mendel needed to see his front gate and strip of lawn and the shingles he had painted himself only two summers before. It was then that the shutters flew open on his very own bedroom window. Mendel turned and ran with all his might, having seen no more of the new resident than a fog of breath. On the next street he found a sewer grate and, with considerable force, yanked it free. A rooster crowed and Mendel heard it at first as a call for help and a siren and the screeching of a bullet. Lowering himself underground and replacing the grate, he heard the rooster's call again and understood what it was— nature functioning as it should. He took it to be another positive sign.

Raising himself from the sewer, Mendel was unsure onto which side of the wall he had emerged. The Ghetto of Chelm was alive with hustle and bustle. Were it not for the ragged appearance of each individual Jew, the crowd could have belonged to any cosmopolitan street.

"What is this? Has the circus returned to Chelm? Have they restocked all the sweetshops with licorice?" Mendel addressed the orphan Yocheved, grabbing hold of her arm and cradling in his palm a tiny potato, which she snatched away. She looked up at him, her eyes wet from the wind.

"We are all going to live on a farm and must hurry not to miss the train."

"A farm you say." He pulled at his beard and bent until his face was even with the child's. "With milking cows?"

"And ducks," said Yocheved before running away.

"Roasted? Or glazed in the style of the Chinese?" he called after her, though she had already disappeared into the crowd, vanishing with the finesse that all the remaining ghetto children had acquired. He had never tasted glazed duck, only knew that there was somewhere in existence such a thing. As he wove through the scrambling ghettoites Mendel fantasized about such a meal, wondered if it was like biting into a caramel-coated apple or as tender and dark as the crust of yolk-basted bread. His stomach churned at the thought of it as he rushed off to find the Rebbe.

The decree was elementary: only essential items were to be taken on the trains. Most packed their meager stores of food, some clothing, and a photograph or two. Here and there a diamond ring found its way into a hunk of bread, or a string of pearls rolled itself into a pair of wool socks.

For the Hasidim of Chelm, interpreting such a request was far from simple. As in any other town where Hasidim live, two distinct groups had formed. In Chelm they were called the Students of the Mekyl and the Mahmir Hasidim. The Students of the Mekyl were a relaxed bunch, taking their worship lightly while keeping within the letter of the law. Due to the ease of observance and the Epicurean way in which they relished in the Lord, they were a very popular group, numbering into the thousands.

The Mahmir Hasidim, on the other hand, were extremely strict. If a fast was to last one day, they would cease eating the day before and starve themselves a day later, guarding against the possibility that in setting their lunar calendars they had been fooled by the phases of the moon. As with the fasts went every requirement in Jewish law. Doubling was not enough, so they tripled, often passing out before pouring the twelfth glass of wine required of the Passover seders. Such zealousness takes much dedication. And considering the adjusted length of the holidays—upward of three weeks at a shot—not any small time commitment either. The Mahmir Hasidim, including children, numbered fewer than twenty on the day the ghetto was dissolved.

Initially circulating as rumor, the edict sparked mass confusion. The inhabitants of the ghetto tried to make logical decisions based on whispers and the skeptical clucking of tongues. Heads of households rubbed their temples and squeezed shut their eyes, struggling to apply their common sense to a situation anything but common.

To ease the terror spreading among his followers, the leader of the Mekyls was forced to make a decree of his own. Hoisted atop a boxcar, balancing on the sawed-off and lovingly sanded broomstick that had replaced his mahogany cane, he defined "essential items" as everything one would need to stock a summer home. In response to a query called out from the crowd of his followers, he announced that the summer home was to be considered unfurnished. He bellowed the last word and slammed down the broomstick for emphasis, sending an echo through the empty belly of the car below.

Off went the Mekyls to gather bedsteads and bureaus,

hammocks and lawn chairs—all that a family might need in relocation. The rabbi of the Mahmir Hasidim, in his infinite strictness (and in response to the shameful indulgence of the Mekyls), understood "essential" to exclude anything other than one's long underwear, for all else was excess adornment.

"Even our ritual fringes?" asked Feitel, astonished.

"Even the hair of one's beard," said the Rebbe, considering the grave nature of their predicament. This sent a shudder through his followers, all except Mendel, who was busy distributing potatoes amid the humble gathering. No one ate. They were waiting for the Rebbe to make the blessing. But the Rebbe refused his share. "Better to give it to a Mekyl who is not so used to doing without."

They all, as if by reflex, stuck out their hands so Mendel should take back theirs too. "Eat, eat!" said the Rebbe. "You eat yours and give me the pleasure of watching." He smiled at his followers. "Such loyal students even Rebbe Akiva, blessed be his memory, would've been honored to have."

The Mahmirim rushed back to their cramped flats, the men shedding their gaberdines and ritual fringes, the women folding their frocks and slipping them into drawers. Feitel, his hand shaking, the tears streaming down his face, began to cut at his beard, bit by bit, inch by inch. "Why not in one shot?" his wife, Zahava, asked. "Get it over with." But he couldn't. So he trimmed at his beard like a barber, as if putting on finishing touches that never seemed right. Zahava paced the floor, stepping through the clumps of hair and the long, dusty rectangles of sunshine that, relentless, could not be kept from the ghetto. For the first time in her married life Zahava left her kerchief at home, needlessly locking the door behind her.

They returned to the makeshift station to find the students of the Mekyl lugging mattresses and dishes and suitcases so full they leaked sleeves and collars from every seam. One little girl brought along her pet dog, its mangy condition made no less shocking by the fact that it looked healthier than its mistress. The Mahmirim turned their faces away from this laxity of definition. An earthly edict, even one coming from their abusers, should be translated strictly lest the invaders think that Jews were not pious in their observance.

The Mahmir Rebbe ordered his followers away from that mass of heathens in case—God forbid—one of the Mahmirim, shivering in long underwear and with naked scalp, should be mistaken for a member of that court. They trudged off in their scanty dress, the women feeling no shame, since the call for such immodesty had come from their teacher's mouth.

Not even the last car of the train was far enough away for the Rebbe. "Come," he said, pushing through the crowd toward the tunnel that was and was not Chelm.

Though there was a track and a tunnel, and a makeshift station newly constructed by the enemy, none of it was actually part of town. Gronam had seen to this himself when the railroad first laid track along the edge of the woods. He had sworn that the train would not pass through any part of Chelm (swore, he thought, safely—sure it wasn't an issue). Checking over maps and deeds and squabbling over whether to pace the distances off heel-toe or toe-heel, the Wise Men discovered that the hill through which the workers were tunneling was very much part of Chelm. They panicked, argued, screamed themselves hoarse in a marathon meeting. It was almost midnight when Gronam came up with a plan.

Tapping on doors, whispering into sleep-clogged ears, the Wise Men roused every able body from bed, and together they sneaked down to the site armed with chisels and kitchen knives, screwdrivers and hoes. It was the only time any of them had been, though only by a few feet, outside of Chelm. Taking up bricks destined for tunnel walls, they waited for Gronam's signal. He *hoo-hoo*ed like an owl and they set to work—etching a longitudinal line around each one. Before dawn, before the workers returned to find the bricks stacked as they were at quitting time the day before and a fine snow of dust around the site, Gronam made a declaration. The top half of every brick was to be considered theirs, and the bottom half, everything below the line, belonged to the railroad. In this way, when the train would enter the tunnel it would not actually pass through Chelm. They reveled in Gronam's wisdom, having kept the railroad out of town and also made its residents richer in the bargain—for they were now the proud owners of so many top halves of bricks which they hadn't had before.

Mendel recalled that morning. He had stood in his nightshirt in the street outside his parents' home and watched his grandfather—the massive Gronam—being carried back to the square on the shoulders of neighbors and friends. Simple times, he thought. Even the greatest of challenges, the battle against the railroad, all seemed so simple now.

The memory left him light-headed (so grueling was the journey from that morning as a child back to the one that, like a trap, bit into their lives with iron teeth). He stumbled forward into the wedge of Mahmirim, nearly knocking little Yocheved to the ground. He steadied himself and then the girl as they moved slowly forward, forging their way across the current of Jews that swirled, rushed, and finally broke against the hard floors of the cattle cars.

Mendel did not understand how the Rebbe planned to reach the tunnel alive, though he believed they would succeed. The darkness had been getting closer for so long, it seemed only just that it should finally envelop them, pull them into its vacuum—the tunnel ready to swallow them up like so many coins dropped into a pocket.

And that is how it felt to Mendel, like they were falling away from an open hand, plunging, as they broke away from the crowd.

In the moment that two guards passed the entrance to the tunnel in opposite directions, their shepherds straining on their leashes, in the moment when the sniper on the top of the train had his attention turned the other way, in the moment before Mendel followed the Rebbe into the tunnel, Yocheved spotted her uncle Misha and froze. Mendel did not bump into her again, though he would, until his death, wish he had.

Yocheved watched her uncle being shoved, brutalized, beaten into a boxcar, her sweet uncle who would carve her treats out of marzipan: flowers, and fruits, and peacocks whose feathers melted on her tongue.

"Come along, Yocheved," the Rebbe called from the tunnel without breaking stride. But the darkness was so uninviting and there was Uncle Misha—a car length away—who always had for her a gift.

Her attention was drawn to the sound of a healthy bark, an angry bark, not the type that might have come from the sickly Jewish dog which had already been put down. It was the bark of a dog that drags its master. Yocheved turned to see the beast bolting along the perimeter of the crowd.

Before the dog could reach her and tear the clothes from her skin and the skin from her bones, the sniper on the train put a single bullet through her neck. The bullet left a ruby hole that resembled a charm an immodest girl might wear. Yocheved touched a finger to her throat and turned her gaze toward the sky, wondering from where such a strange gift had come.

Only Mendel looked back at the sound of the shot; the others had learned the lessons of Sodom.

The Mahmirim followed the tracks around a bend where they found, waiting for them, a passenger train. Maybe a second train waited outside every ghetto so that Mahmirim should not have to ride with Mekylim. The cars were old, a patchwork of relics from the last century. The locomotive in the distance looked too small for the job. Far better still, Mendel felt, than the freight wagons and the chaos they had left on the other side of the tunnel. Mendel was sure that the conductor waited for the next train at the next ghetto to move on with its load. There had never been enough travel or commerce to warrant another track and suddenly there was traffic, so rich was the land with Jews.

"Nu?" the Rebbe said to Mendel. "You are the tallest. Go have a look."

At each car, Mendel placed his foot on the metal step and pulled himself up with the bar bolted alongside. His hands were huge, befitting his lineage. Gronam's own were said to have been as broad as a shovel's head. Mendel's—somewhat smaller—had always been soft, ungainly but unnoticed. The ghetto changed that. It turned them hard and menacing. There was a moment as he grabbed hold of the bar when the Mahmirim wondered if Mendel would rise up to meet the window or pull the train over on their heads.

Leaning right, peering in, Mendel announced his findings. "Full," he said. "Full." Then "Full, again." Pressed together as one, the Rebbe and his followers moved forward after each response.

On the fourth attempt the car was empty and Mendel pushed open the door. The Mahmirim hurried aboard, still oblivious to their good fortune and completely unaware that it was a gentile train.

On any other transport the Mahmirim wouldn't have gotten even that far. But this happened to be a train of showmen, entertainers waiting for clear passage to a most important engagement. These were worldly people traveling about during wartime. Very little in the way of oddities could shock them—something in which they took great pride. And, of course, as Mendel would later find out, there had been until most recently the Romanian and his bear. Because of him—and the bear—those dozing in the last few cars, those who saw the flash of Mendel's head and the pack of identically clad fools stumbling behind, were actually tickled at the sight. Another lesson in fate for Mendel. The difference between the sniper's bullet and survival fell somewhere between a little girl's daydream and a fondness for bears.

The Romanian had been saddled with a runtish second-hand bear that would not dance or step up on a ball or growl with fake ferociousness. Useless from a life of posing with children in front of a slack-shuttered camera, the bear refused to do anything but sit. From this the Romanian concocted a routine. He would dress the bear as a wounded soldier and lug his furry comrade around the stage, setting off firecrackers and spouting political satire. It brought audiences to hysterics. A prize act! From this he came up with others: the fireman, the side-splitting Siamese twins, and—for the benefit of the entertainers themselves—the bride. When the train was chugging slowly up a hill, the Romanian would dress the bear in bridal gown and veil. He'd get off the front car cradling his bride and pretend they'd just missed their honeymoon train to the mountains. The entertainers howled with joy as he ran alongside the tracks crying out for a conductor and tripping over a giant tin pocket watch tied to his waist and dragging behind. A funny man, that Romanian. And strong. A very strong man it takes to run with a bear.

When the Mahmirim appeared at the back of the train, all who saw them remembered their friend. How they all missed his antics after he was taken away. And how the little bear had moped. Like a real person. Yes, it would be good to have a new group of wiseacres. And they turned in their seats, laughing out loud at these shaved-headed fools, these clowns without makeup—no, not clowns, acrobats. They could only be acrobats in such bland and colorless attire—and so skinny, too. Just the right builds for it. Lithe for the high wire.

In this way, the Mahmirim successfully boarded the train.

They busied themselves with choosing compartments, seeing that Raizel the widow had space to prop up her feet, separating the women from the men, trying to favor husbands and wives and to keep the youngest, Shraga, a boy of eleven, with his mother. In deference to King Saul's having numbered the people with lambs, the Rebbe, as is the fashion, counted his followers with a verse of Psalms, one word for each person, knowing already that he would fall short without Yocheved. This is the curse that had befallen them. Always one less word.

Mendel, who had once been a Mekyl but overcome by the wisdom of the Mahmirim had joined their small tribe, still hadn't lost his taste for excessive drink. He found his way to the bar car—well stocked for wartime—without even a pocket, let alone a złoty, with which he might come by some refreshment. Scratching at the wool of his long underwear, he stared at the bottles, listening as they rocked one against the other, tinkling lightly like chimes. He was especially taken with a leaded-crystal decanter. Its smooth single-malt contents rode up and down its inner walls, caressing the glass and teasing Mendel in a way that he considered cruel.

Dismissing the peril to which he was exposing the others, Mendel sought out a benefactor who might sport him a drink. It was in this way—in which only God can turn a selfish act into a miracle—that Mendel initially saved all of their lives.

An expert on the French horn complimented Mendel on the rustic simplicity of his costume and invited him to join her in a drink. It was this tippler who alerted Mendel to the fact that the Mahmirim were assumed to be acrobats. Talking freely, and intermittently cursing the scheduling delays caused by the endless transports, she told him of the final destinations of those nuisance-causing trains.

"This," she said, "was told to me by Günter the Magnificent—who was never that magnificent considering that Druckenmüller always outclassed him with both the doves and the rings." She paused and ordered two brandies. Mendel put his hand out to touch her arm, stopping short of contact.

"If you wouldn't mind, if it's not too presumptuous." He pointed to the decanter, blushing, remembering the Rebbe's lectures on gluttony.

"Fine choice, fine choice. My pleasure." She knocked an empty snifter against the deep polished brown of the table (a color so rich it seemed as if the brandy had seeped through her glass and distilled into the table's surface). Not since the confiscation of the Mekyl Rebbe's cane had Mendel seen such opulence. "Barman, a scotch as well. Your finest." The barman served three drinks and the musician poured the extra brandy into her glass. She drank without a word. Mendel toasted her silently and, after the blessing, sipped at his scotch, his first in so very long. He let its smoky flavor rise up and fill his head, hoping that if he drank slowly enough, if he let the scotch rest on his tongue long enough and roll gradually enough down his throat, then maybe he could cure his palate like the oak slats of a cask. Maybe then he could keep the warmth and the comfort with him for however much longer God might deem that they should survive.

"Anyway, Günter came to us directly from a performance for the highest of the high where his beautiful assistant Leine had been told in the powder room by the wife of an official of unmatched feats of magic being performed with the trains. They go away full—packed so tightly that babies are stuffed in over the heads of the passengers when there's no room for another full grown—and come back empty, as if never before used."

"And the Jews?" asked Mendel. "What trick is performed with the Jews?"

"Sleight of hand," she said, splashing the table with her drink and waving her fingers by way of demonstration. "A classic illusion. First they are here, and then they are gone.

"According to the wife of the official, those who witness it faint dead away, overcome by the grand scale of the illusion. For a moment the magician stands, a field of Jews at his feet, then nothing." She paused for dramatic effect, not unaccustomed to life in the theater. "The train sits empty. The magician stands alone on the platform. Nothing remains but the traditional puff of smoke. This trick he performs, puff after puff, twenty-four hours a day.

"After Günter heard, he forgot all about Druckenmüller and his doves and became obsessed with what Leine had told him. He would sit at the bar and attempt the same thing with rabbits, turning his ratty bunnies into colored bursts of smoke, some pink, some purple, occasionally plain gray. He swore he wouldn't give up until he had perfected his magic. Though he knew, you could tell, that it would never match the magnitude of a trainload of Jews. I told him myself when he asked my opinion. Günter, I said, it takes more than nimble fingers to achieve the extraordinary." With that Mendel felt a hand on his knee.

Pausing only to finish his drink, Mendel ran back to the car full of Mahmirim and relayed to the Rebbe the tales of horror he had heard. Mendel was the Rebbe's favorite. Maybe not always so strict in his service of the Lord, Mendel was full of His spirit; this the Rebbe could see. For that reason he ignored the prohibition against gossip and took into consideration his student's most unbelievable report.

"It can't be, Mendele!" said the Rebbe.

"Their cruelty knows no bounds," cried Raizel the widow.

The Rebbe sat in silence for some minutes, considering the

events of the last years and the mystery of all those who had disappeared before them. He decided that what Mendel told them must be so.

"I'm afraid," he said, "that the gossip Mendel repeats is true. Due to its importance, in this instance there can be no sin in repeating such idle talk." The Rebbe glanced at the passing scenery and pulled at the air where once had been his beard. "No other choice," he said. "A solitary option. Only one thing for us to do . . ." The followers of the Mahmir Rebbe hung on his words.

"We must tumble."

Mendel had been to the circus as a boy. During the three-day engagement, Mendel had sneaked into the tent for every performance, hiding under the bowed pine benches and peering out through the space beneath all the legs too short to reach the hay-strewn ground.

Though he did not remember a single routine or feat of daring, he did recall, in addition to the sparkling of some scandalously placed sequins, the secret to convincing the other performers that they were indeed acrobats. The secret was nothing more than an exclamation. It was, simply, a "Hup!" Knowing this, the Mahmirim lined the corridor and began to practice.

"You must clap your hands once in a while as well," Mendel told them. The Rebbe was already nearing old age and therefore clapped and hupped far more than he jumped.

Who knew that Raizel the widow had double-jointed arms, or that Shmuel Berel could scurry about upside down on hands and feet mocking the movements of a crab. Falling from a luggage rack from which he had tried to suspend himself, Mendel, on his back, began to laugh. The others shared the release and laughed along with him. In their car near the end of the train, there was real and heartfelt delight. They were giddy with the chance God had granted them. They laughed as the uncondemned might, as free people in free countries do.

The Rebbe interrupted this laughter. "Even in the most foreign situation we must adhere to the laws," he said. Therefore, as in the laws of singing, no woman was to tumble unless accompanied by another woman, and no man was to catch a woman—though husbands were given a dispensation to catch their airborne wives.

Not even an hour had gone by before it was obvious what state they were in: weak with hunger and sickness, never having asked of their bodies such rigors before—all this on top of their near-total ignorance of acrobatics and the shaking of the train. At the least, they would need further direction. A tip or two on which to build.

Pained by the sight of it, the Rebbe called a stop to their futile flailing about.

"Mendel," he said, "back to your drunks and gossips. Bring us the secrets to this act. As is, not even a blind man would be tricked by the sounds of such graceless footfalls."

"Me!" Mendel said, with the mock surprise of Moses, as if there were some other among them fit to do the job.

"Yes, you," the Rebbe said, shooing him away. "Hurry off."

Mendel did not move.

He looked at the Mahmirim as he thought the others might. He saw that it was only by God's will that they had gotten that far. A ward of the insane or of consumptives would have been a far better misperception in which to entangle this group of uniformly clad souls. Their acceptance as acrobats was a stretch, a first-glance guess, a benefit of the doubt granted by circumstance and only as valuable as their debut would prove. It was an absurd undertaking. But then again, Mendel thought, no more unbelievable than the reality from which they'd escaped, no more unfathomable than the magic of disappearing Jews. If the good people of Chelm could believe that water was sour cream, if the peasant who woke up that first morning in Mendel's bed and put on Mendel's slippers and padded over to the window could believe, upon throwing back the shutters, that the view he saw had always been his own, then why not pass as acrobats and tumble across the earth until they found a place where they were welcome?

"What am I to bring back?" Mendel said.

"The secrets," answered the Rebbe, an edge in his voice, no time left for hedging or making things clear. "There are secrets behind everything that God creates."

"And a needle and thread," said Raizel the widow. "And a pair of scissors. And anything, too."

"Anything?" Mendel said.

"Yes, anything," Raizel said. "Bits of paper or string. Anything that a needle can prick or thread can hold."

Mendel raised his eyebrows at the request. The widow talked as if he were heading off to Cross-eyed Bilha's general store.

"They will have," she said. "They are entertainers—forever losing buttons and splitting seams." She clucked her tongue at Mendel, who still had his eyebrows raised. "These costumes, as is, will surely never do."

It was the horn gleaming on the table next to the slumped form of its player that first caught Mendel's attention. He rushed over and sat down next to her. He stared out the window at the forest rushing by. He tried to make out secluded worlds cloaked by the trees. Little Yocheved's farm must be out there somewhere, a lone homestead hidden like Eden in the woods. It would be on the other side of a broad and rushing river where the dogs would lose scent of a Jewish trail.

Mendel knocked on the table to rouse the musician and looked up to find gazes focused upon him from around the bar. The observers did not appear unfriendly, only curious, travel weary, interested—Mendel assumed—in a new face who already knew a woman so well.

"You?" she said, lifting her head and smiling. "My knight in bedclothes has returned." The others went back to their drinks as she scanned the room in half consciousness. "Barman," she called. "A drink for my knight." She rested her head on the crook of her arm and slid the horn over so she could see Mendel with an uninterrupted view. "You were in my dream," she said. "You and Günter. I mustn't tell such stories anymore, they haunt me so."

"I've torn my costume," Mendel said, "the only one I have. And in a most embarrassing place."

Shielded by the table, she walked her fingers up Mendel's leg.

"I can't imagine where," she said, attempting a flutter of alcohol-deadened lids.

"Thread," Mendel said, "and a needle. You wouldn't happen to have—"

"Of course," she said. She tried to push herself up. "In my compartment, come along. I'll sew you up there."

"No," he said. "You go, I'll stay here—and if you could, if you wouldn't mind making an introduction, I'm in desperate need of advice."

"After I sew you," she said. She curled her lip into a pout, accentuating an odd mark left by years of playing. "It's only two cars away."

"You go," Mendel said. "And then we'll talk. And maybe later tonight I'll come by and you can reinforce the seams." Mendel winked.

The horn player purred and went off, stumbling against the rhythm of the train so that she actually appeared balanced. Mendel spied the open horn case under the table. Rummaging through it, he found a flowered cotton rag, damp with saliva. Looking about, nonchalant, he tucked it into his sleeve.

"It's called a Full Twisting Voltas," Mendel said, trying to approximate the move as he had understood it. Aware that, as much as had been lost during a half demonstration in a smoke-filled bar car, twice that was again lost in his return to the Mahmirim, and another twice that lost again in his body's awkward translation of the move.

Shmuel Berel, intent and driven, attempted the move first, proving—as he would throughout the afternoon—to be almost completely useless when it came to anything where timing was involved. Under protest, for he wanted to do his share, Shmuel was told to scuttle about the stage continuously during the performance doing his upside-down backward walk. Coordination proved to be a problem for Raizel the widow and Shraga's mother, and—not surprisingly—the Rebbe as well. For them Mendel returned again to the bar car in search of simpler, less challenging moves. For Shraga, a live wire and a natural performer, he inquired about some more complicated combinations on which to work.

Mendel paused between cars, pondering the rush of track and tie and the choices it raised. How would it be if he were to jump off and roll, in faulty acrobatic form, down an embankment and into a stretch of field? What if he were to start himself off on another tributary of the nightmare, to seek out a scheme as random and hopeless as the one of which he was a part; and what of the wheels and the possibility of lowering himself underneath, thrusting himself into some new hell that would at least guarantee a comfort in its permanence—how much easier to face an eternity without wonder? Over and over again, Mendel chose neither, feeling the rush of wind and moving on into the next car, passing and excusing, smiling his way along, his senses sharpened like a nesting bird's, eagle-eyed and watching for scraps of cotton or lost ribbon, anything to bring back to Raizel and her needle.

Two men, forever at the same window and smoking a ransom's worth of cigars, had come to recognize Mendel and begun to make friendly jokes at his expense. The pair particularly relished the additions to his costume. "The Ragdoll Review," one would say. And the other, rotating the cigar, puff, puff, puffing away at it like a locomotive himself, would yank it from his mouth and say, "How many of you are there, each adorned with one more scrap?"

As many as the cars, Mendel thought, and the trains, and the lengths of track. As many as have been taken and wait at the stations and right now move toward another place. As plentiful as the drops of rain that puddle the world over, except in Chelm, where they gather in the gutters into torrents of sour cream.

Each time Mendel returned to the Mahmirim, he found the car seemingly empty. At most he'd catch a rustling of curtains, or find Raizel smiling sheepishly—too slow to seal herself into a compartment before his entrance. It reminded him of the center of town when strangers stumbled through. All the townspeople would disappear, including Cross-eyed Bilha, who also ran the inn. (The inn was a brainchild of the Wise Men—for whether or not strangers were welcome, no one should be able to say that Chelm was so provincial as to lack accommodations.) Eventually, out of curiosity or terror, a resident who could stand the suspense no longer would venture a look outside. The circus, prepared for a three-day extravaganza, whip and chair already in the ring and tigers poised on overturned tubs, had sat three times three days until one of the Wise Men first dared peer into the tent.

"Open up," Mendel called, "it gets dark and there's work to be done." Compartment doors opened and Mendel told everyone to remain in their seats. "Just Shraga," he said, "and Feitel and Zahava. We are going to break the routine down into sections, and each will learn his own part."

"No," the Rebbe said. "There isn't time. What if we should arrive in an hour before all have learned what it is they are to do?"

"There is time," Mendel said. "The train barely moves now. Up front they get off and walk alongside only to climb on a few lengths back. We will have the whole of tomorrow morning and up until noon. The horn player told me—we are headed to an evening performance."

"It sounds like they are trying to make a fool of you," Feitel said. "As if maybe they know."

"Do they know?" Zahava asked.

"What is it they know?" Little Shraga came out of his compartment, frightened.

"No one knows," Mendel said. "If they knew it would be over and done with—of that you can be sure. As for practicing, there is great wisdom in the sections. They will allow you to rest, Rebbe, and for Raizel to sew." Mendel smiled at Raizel as she fastened a cork to Feitel's chest. Feitel chewed on a bit of thread to keep away the Angel of Death, for only the dead wear their garments while they are sewn. "It is called choreography, Rebbe. It is the way such things are done."

That understood, they worked on the choreography in the aisle that ran the length of the car. Those watching sat in their compartments with the doors slid open and tried to pick up the moves from the quick flicker of a body in motion passing before them. It was like learning how to dance by thumbing through a flip book, page by page.

While some worked on cartwheels and somersaults, rolling in a line first one way and then the other, Shraga, reckless and with more room in which to move his spindly body, actually showed a great deal of promise. So much that the Rebbe said, "In another world, my son, who knows what might have become of you."

The Mahmirim worked until they could work no more. That night they rolled in their sleep while the engineer up front tugged his whistle in greeting to the engines pulling the doomed the other way.

Shraga was the first to rise, an hour before dawn. He woke each of the others with a gentle touch on the shoulder. Each one, snapping awake, looked around for a moment, agitated and confused.

They began to practice right off, doing the best they could in the darkness. The Rebbe interrupted as the sky began to lighten. "Come up from there," the Rebbe said to Raizel. She was on the floor tearing bits of upholstery from under the seats, from where the craftsmen had cinched the corners. These she would sew into a moon over Zahava's heart. "Come along," the Rebbe said. Mendel, who was fiddling with a spoon Raizel had fastened to a sleeve and advising Shraga on the length of his leap, came with the others to crowd around the Rebbe's compartment.

"More than one kind of dedication is required if we are to survive this ordeal." The Rebbe looked out the window as he spoke.

They separated the men from the women and began to say their morning prayers. It was not a matter of disregarding the true peril to which it exposed them but an instance in which the danger was not considered. They called out to the heavens in full voices. When they had finished there was a pause, a moment of silence. It was as if they were waiting for an answer from the Lord.

. . .

The train stopped.

Feitel was in the air when it did. He landed with a momentum greater than the train's and rolled pell-mell into the hardness of a wall.

"I've broken my back," he said. The others ignored him. There wasn't the urgency of truth in his voice. And outside the windows there were tracks upon tracks and platform after platform and the first uncountable stories of a building, higher, surely, than the Tower of Babel was ever meant to be.

By the time Feitel got to his feet, the performers had already begun to pour out onto the platform, lugging trunks and valises, garment bags and makeup cases with rounded edges and silver clasps.

The door to the car slammed open and a head and shoulders popped in. On the face was a thin mustache that, like a rain gutter, diverted the sweat away from pale lips. And how the sweat ran; in that very first moment the face reddened noticeably and new beads of perspiration drove on the last.

"Who are you?" the man asked. "What might this ragtag bunch perform?"

Mendel stepped forward.

"We are the tumblers."

"Have you tumbled off the garbage heap?"

Feitel felt the ridiculousness of his costume and put his hand over the five-pointed star of champagne corks fastened to his chest.

"No matter," the man said. "How much prep time do you need?"

"Prep?" Mendel was at a loss.

"I've no patience for this. We're three hours late already. They'll have my head, not yours." A hand plunged through the door. The man looked at the watch on the wrist and wiped the sweat from his brow as best he could. The hand appeared an odd match, as if this intruder were constructed of loose parts. His face reddened further and he puffed out his cheeks. "Prep time," he said. "Trampolines, pommel horses, trapezes. What needs be set up?"

"Nothing," Mendel said.

"As plain as you look, eh? Fine. Then, good." He appeared to calm slightly—ever so slightly. "Then you're on first. Now get down there and help the others lug their chattel to the theater."

The Mahmirim rushed out the door, Mendel's mouth opening wide as he followed the rest of the building into the sky. He let out a whistle and then continued to gape. It was beautiful and menacing. The whole place was menacing, for every wonder was in some way marred, every thing of beauty stained gray with war. To try to escape from it, to schedule galas and dress for balls, was farcical even for the enemy. The gray mood was all pervading. The performers hurried along with their preshow expressions, looking dyspeptic. Impostors, one and all. Their stage smiles, Mendel knew, would sparkle.

Raizel the widow led a monkey on a leash. The monkey held a banana, the first any had seen in years. The widow would pick up her pace and then stop suddenly. The monkey did the same. Her crooked fingers were bunched into a single claw, ready to snatch the prize away at first chance. Mendel stood behind her, a trunk on his head, watching Raizel try to trick a banana from a monkey. He was surprised, as always, to witness a new degradation, to find another display of wretchedness original enough to bring tears to his eyes. He took a deep breath and ignored his sense of injustice, a rich man's emotion, a feeling Mendel had given up the liberty of experiencing horrors and horrors before.

. . .

It was only a short time until they reached their destination, a building as wide as the train was long. The interior promised to be grand. But the Mahmirim didn't get to see any of the trompe l'oeil or gold leaf that adorned the lobby. They were ushered backstage through double doors.

As the procession filed in, the mood of the entertainers transformed. There was a newfound energy, a heightened professionalism. Even the drinkers from the bar car and the tired smokers Mendel had shuffled past in the passageways moved with a sudden precision. Mendel took note of it as a juggler grabbed the monkey and began, with detached brutality, to force the animal into trousers. He noted it as the aging dancers hid their heads behind the lids of mirrored cases, only to look up again having created an illusion of youth that, from any seat in the house, would go unchallenged. Mendel went cold with terror, watching, trying to isolate what in these innocuous preparations was so disturbing.

As the stage manager hurried by, his shirt transparent with perspiration, his arms full of tin swords, and screaming "Schnell" at anyone whose idle gaze he caught, Mendel understood to what his great terror was due. It was the efficiency displayed by each and every one, the crack hop-to-it-ness, the discipline and order. He had seen it from the start, from the day the intruders marched into town and, finding the square empty, began kicking down doors, from the instant meticulousness demanded that a war of such massive scope make time to seek out a happily isolated dot-on-the-map hamlet-called-city where resided the fools of Chelm. It was this efficiency, Mendel knew, that would catch up with them.

"It's like we are in the bowels of the earth," Raizel said, motioning to the catwalk and the sandbags and the endless ropes and pegs.

"Which one to pull for rain?" Feitel said. "And which for a good harvest?"

"And which for redemption?" the Rebbe said—his tone forlorn and as close as he came to despair.

"You did a wonderful job," Mendel said. He, against all they had been taught, put a hand to Raizel's cheek. "The costumes are most imaginative." He knocked his elbows together, and the spoons clinked like a dull chime.

"A wonder with a needle and thread. It's true." This from Zahava in a breastplate of cigarette boxes and with pipe cleaners sewn to her knees.

The widow slipped an arm around Zahava's waist—always such a trim girl, even before—and pulled her close as she used to do Sabbath mornings on the way out of the shtibl. Raizel squeezed her as tightly as she could, and Zahava, more gently, squeezed back. Both held their eyes closed. It was obvious that they were together in another place, back outside the shtibl when the dogwoods were in bloom, both in new dresses, modest and lovely.

Mendel and the Rebbe and Feitel, all the Mahmirim who could not join in the embrace or the escape to better times, looked away. It was too much to bear unopaqued by any of the usual defenses. They raised their eyes as Zahava planted a kiss on the old woman's head, a kiss so sincere that Mendel tried to cut the gravity by half:

"You know," he said, "never has so much been made of the accidental boarding of a second-class train."

His observation, a poor joke, did not get a single smile. It only set the Mahmirim to looking about once again, desperate for a place on which to rest their gazes.

It may have come from a leaky pipe, a hole in the roof, or off the chin of the stage manager darting about, but most likely it was a tear abandoned by an anonymous eye. It hit the floor, a single drop, immediately to the right of the Rebbe.

"What is this?" the Rebbe said. "I won't have it. Not for a minute!"

Mendel and the others put on expressions as if they did not

know to what he referred, as if they did not sense the somberness and the defeat rising up around them.

"Come, come," said the Rebbe. "We are on first, and Shraga has not yet perfected his Full Twisting Voltas." He tapped out a four beat with his foot. "Hup," he said. "From the top," he said, exhausting all of the vocabulary that he had learned.

They made a space for themselves and ran through the routine, the Rebbe not letting them rest for a moment and Mendel loving him with all his heart.

The manager came for them at five minutes to curtain. It was then, from the wings, that they got to see it all. The red carpets and festooned gold braids, the chandelier and frescoed ceiling—full of heroes and maidens and celestial rays—hemmed in by elaborate moldings. And the moldings themselves were bedecked with rosy-cheeked cherubim carved from wood. There was also the audience—the women in gowns and hair piled high, the men in their uniforms, pinned heavy with medals for efficiency and bravery and strength. An important audience, just the kind to make a nervous man sweat. There was also a box up and off to the left; in it sat a leader and his escort, a man of great power on whom, Mendel could tell, a part of everyone was focused. The chandelier was turned down and the stage lights came up and the manager whispered "Go" so that Shraga stepped out onto the stage. The others followed. It was as plain as that. They followed because there was nothing else to do.

For a moment, then two, then three, they all stood at the back of the stage, blinded. Raizel put a hand up to her eyes. There was a cough and then a chuckle. The echo had not yet come to rest when the Rebbe called out:

"To your marks!"

Lifting their heads, straightening their postures, they spread out across the hard floor.

"Hup," cried the Rebbe, and the routine commenced.

Shraga cartwheeled and flipped. The widow Raizel jumped once and then stood off to the side with her double-jointed arms turned inside out. Mendel, glorious Mendel, actually executed a springing Half-Hanlon and, with Shmuel Berel's assistance (his only real task), ended in a Soaring Angel. Feitel, off his mark, missed his wife as she came toward him in a leap. Zahava landed on her ankle, which let out a crisp, clear crack. She did not whimper, quickly standing up. Though it was obvious even from the balcony that her foot was not on right. There was, after a gasp from the audience, silence. Then from above, from off to the left, a voice was heard. Mendel knew from which box it came. He knew it was the most polished, the most straight and tall, a maker of magic, to be sure. Of course, this is conjecture, for how could he see?

"Look," said the voice. "They are as clumsy as Jews." There was a pause and then singular and boisterous laughter. The laughter echoed and was picked up by the audience, who laughed back with lesser glee—not wanting to overstep their bounds. Mendel looked back to the Rebbe, and the Rebbe shrugged. Young Shraga, a natural survivor, took a hop-step as if to continue. Zahava moved toward the widow Raizel and rested a hand on her shoulder.

"More," called the voice. "The farce can't have already come to its end. More!" it said. Another voice, that of a woman, came from the same place and barely carried to the stage.

"Yes, keep on," it said. "More of the Jewish ballet." The fatuous laugh that followed, as with the other, was picked up by the audience and the cavernous echo so that it seemed even the wooden cherubim laughed from above.

The Rebbe took a deep breath and began to tap with his foot.

Mendel waved him off and stepped forward, moving downstage, the spotlight harsh and unforgiving against his skin. He reached out past the footlights into the dark, his hands cracked and bloodless, gnarled and intrusive.

Mendel turned his palms upward, benighted.

But there were no snipers, as there are for hands that reach out of the ghettos; no dogs, as for hands that reach out from the cracks in boxcar floors; no angels waiting, as they always do, for hands that reach out from chimneys into ash-clouded skies.

Reunion

The house has an odd smell to it, an odor. The rabbi's got thirteen kids and that's the smell. The constant cycling of daily needs. Someone always eating or shitting, putting on socks or taking them off. But it's not white like on the ward. Not sterile and faked. It's real life over there with the smells that go with it.

Marty is saying this himself, explaining it to another patient in the dayroom as he grinds out a cigarette and picks a bit of tobacco from his tongue.

Marty feels at home on the ward. Both his children had been born there when it was maternity, before they changed it all around and put in the steel doors. You can't wipe away that kind of feeling, though, the joy of births and new lives, of daughters and sons. Maybe that's why they keep the mentals there now, to give the place a metaphysical boost—let them recuperate on a ward with hope-soaked, life-affirming walls.

He treats the place as if it were a country club, dressing in expensive, casual slacks and loafers, pressed shirts and V-neck sweaters that give off more of a feeling of money than would jackets and ties. He plays the part as well. Acts as if, as long as he can't get back to his golf game, he might as well make the best of it, smiling at the other patients, shaking hands, quipping and winking, and laughing through his nose whenever the chance arises.

The staff favors Marty and encourages the new friendship he's made.

A John Doe is picked up off the street of a neighboring suburb in the midst of a violent rage; he is rolled onto the ward strapped to a gurney, fighting to free his wrists from the canvas bands or tear his hands off trying.

The nurses land a needle in his thigh.

Then Marty, big man on the ward, wanders into Doe's room as a pair of nurses is removing the restraints. With a finger keeping place in a hardcover biography, Marty leans over, peers into Doe's drugged face, and says, "I could swear we've met. Is it possible that you were here with me last spring?"

And Doe answers a moment later, maybe two. "No," he says, "I don't believe I was."

Most of the nurses and all the rest of the patients are afraid of Doe. But Marty has found in him a huge, brooding confidant. A willing ear. Doe is not outwardly compassionate or wise, but the companionship is enough. For Marty has a lot to say and not enough time to say it with the thoughts coming so fast and the drugs slowing Marty down.

"Like having a honeycomb in my head," he says. "A geometric form with every side as much up as down. Soon as I have my feet firmly planted, I discover I'm sideways—and all the other slopes looking flat as floor."

When Doe is preoccupied, when he nods off or is simply caught in his own head, Marty pictures himself moving from chamber to chamber, walking up walls like Fred Astaire. Taking these odd angles on and seeing where they go.

Sometimes it is the plate falling and falling and falling. A satellite. His moon. Marty at home with his family watching himself, watching the plate, watching everything go terribly wrong.

Then there is shul, him reaching, the gabbai yelling. The Torah falling and unfurling and spreading outward like a red carpet, black word after word after word.

Doe is street-ugly. That is, not unhandsome naturally, but his nose has had breaks, and there are old scars and new sores, a tangle of beard, and a dangerous look that is always there so that even if Doe is stumbled upon sleeping behind a Dumpster a person is forced to think twice. And the nurses do. They double up always, especially for late-night check-ins, when, considering how deeply they sedate him, it is a precaution more easily attributed to fear of the dark.

Marty, on the other hand, arrived at the nurses' station ready to sign himself in with a whole set of Italian-make hardcase luggage in tow.

Marjorie, the head nurse, knows him of course. He is in and out more and more often over the years. The cycles speed up that way with age. "The wife," he says, shrugging. He is there for Robin, as a favor to her.

The nurses are prejudiced against this wife. Their patients are not generally debonair and handsome in a way that makes the heart rush. When she arrives to make sure Marty is in, they see a little woman, drawn and tired in her cheap blouses and A&S shoes. Robin has no smiles or anecdotes, no warmth for them. After she leaves they wonder if she cuts her own hair.

This time, as soon as the wife left, Marty put a case up on the counter and popped it open, *click* and then *click*. So staged in his motions, so dramatic, still talking while he rifled through. "Looks like I've been making scenes again. Seems I've stretched the family budget a bit too far." Pulling back his arm, he said, "Here it is. A gift for you, Marjorie." He lowered the case, passed her a ribboned and bowed box. A younger nurse blushed. "In Milan," he said, "I had a feeling that we'd be seeing each other, thought I might be back this way soon. Fine leathers," he said, "fine women. Fine weather. A beautiful country. You should try and get there this time of year."

"Tell Robin you were thinking of *her* in Milan," Marjorie said, handing back the gift. "Now why don't you get set up. Nurse Williams will take you to your room." Marjorie would have none of it. She never did. In the past, other nurses had been more susceptible to his flattery. There was one, once, back a while, that had been dismissed. She had been seen straightening the seams of her white stockings as she made her way out of his room.

"A chopped-liver moon," Marty says, "if I had to freeze it, freeze the moment when I knew it'd gone wrong. I walked into the house after synagogue, same as always. Table set, wine and challah, four small plates of liver, each with a little slice of carrot on top. Hardly in the room a second and the plate is up in the air, headed toward me. And there's this moment when I'm watching it high in its trajectory, hanging in an arc over the table. Robin's looking at it, the kids are looking up at it, we're all watching this plate hanging there. A perfect little moon that is all the sadness and anger that is my home." Marty bites at a nail, looking off. "Once the dishes start to fly, it's not long until I'm back in here." He turns to Doe. "Something's gone very wrong in my life."

"Better in here," Doe says. "Something goes right if I'm in here."

"Nah," Marty tells him. "You don't mean that. Loving the kids so much, my Leah and my Sammy, loving Robin the way I do, it's only trouble. You did it right for people like us. Living on the street. Free. Cut loose."

"Cut myself loose," Doe says. "But I didn't drift very far."

. . .

The children, Leah and Sammy, had beat him home from services. Marty had taken his time, strolling down Walnut and thinking to himself all the things he should have said. He had stepped into the dining room muttering a righteous speech, and Robin, raging, had thrown a small Corning Ware dish at his head. It shattered on the wall and he felt the splinters against his neck. She threw a glass and it hit the wall with greater force. Marty touched a finger behind his ear and there was blood. Leah screamed, "Ima!"

"Go now," Robin said, "anywhere. Just go. Disappear or I'll have to kill you for what you do to this family. I'll stab you to death right here in front of the children and that will really ruin their lives." Leah caught her mother's glance toward the table and grabbed for the serrated challah knife on the cutting board. "Unnecessary, dear, I'm going to use a butcher knife. I'm going to stab your father through the heart, not saw off his head."

"Ima!" Leah screamed, holding it long so that her voice broke and the tendons in her neck went taut. "Ima, don't," she screamed, dropping to her knees. Sammy did not scream, did not say anything. And if his mother had wanted to get a meat knife from the kitchen, he would have stepped aside and let her pass.

"Robin would have left me long ago if it weren't for the rabbi. The master of forgiveness. He can explain anything away.

"Not so much what he says, either. But his style. The example he sets. A good man, the rabbi. Always ready to roll up his sleeves to save a Jewish marriage. Sits behind his big desk in front of a mint's worth of silver picture frames. Talks about peace in the home in his high girl's voice, with that sweet stink of a smell in the air. And Robin can't get away. My wife's helpless inside that house, with a football team at breakfast, lunch, and dinner, and the place running like a machine. If they can pull that off, what's Robin got to say? Two lovely children and a problem husband are too much? The rabbi and his wife have a baker's dozen: two of them slow and one with leg braces, clanking around the house like the Tin Man."

"My brother," Doe says. "My brother is the rabbi of your shul." Doe takes a long, long pause, looking past Marty. He gives a short sigh. "Maybe," he says.

Marty is leaning forward in his chair, rubbing both palms in circles against his knees. He heard it right. Not the claim, but the word. "Shul" is what Doe said. Not "temple" or "synagogue," but "shul."

"What do you mean 'rabbi'?" Marty asks.

"Over at Ohav Shalom. In Bridgelawn."

The silence is Marty's this time. He's considering. The delivery was sincere. But they are short on sanity, not sincerity, on the ward. There is the old lady with rouge caked on her cheeks who stands patiently by the nurses' station, a paper flower taped to her wrist and waiting for her prom date to arrive. There is the tiring textbook schizoid who thinks the CIA is out to get him, and another patient who corresponds with her dead daughter and the drowned star Natalie Wood. She writes them joint letters—fully aware they never write back. Each of these people is sincere as can be. And now Doe: "My brother is your rabbi." Doe, Marty's good listener. Like the rabbi. Doe, his friend. Marty looks, studies, decides in a flash.

"Of course," Marty yells, and brings down an open palm on the low table. "I knew I knew you," he says. "Did I not say so from the start? Your last name, what is it, after all?"

"Baum," Doe says. And Baum it is. Rabbi Baum of Bridge-lawn.

"You're lying," Marty says; his smile is broad.

"Not in for lying, if they locked up liars . . ."

Marty lets out a yelp, starts to stand, sits, gives the table another slap.

"I'll be damned. So that's where I know you from. From the pull to your eyes, and the way you walk. I know your genes. I recognize the prominent strands of Baum DNA." A nurse comes by to check on the noise. Marty stands, puts a hand on Doe's shoulder. "Did I not say it? Did I not say this man looked familiar?" He pinches a cheek. "Did I not from day one recognize a classic Baum face?"

On the night of the broken dishes, Marty went away to anywhere. To Milan.

When he returned, when he walked through the door with the Connecticut Limousine driver following, carrying in case after beautiful case, Robin, after thirty-one days of cooldown, said, "A real piece of work, you are."

"You told me to disappear."

"And to steal my credit card?"

"You cut mine up. And being you is so easy. Is it my fault you have a flexible name?"

"Madman's logic," she said.

"I brought gifts."

Robin blocked the driver as he came in with a trunk. "Back out," she said, "wrong address. To Five Cedars. To the loony bin." Like she was sending them out for milk, or a video, out to cruise the quiet streets searching for the kids' lost dog.

"For real?" the driver said.

"No joke," Robin told him. She turned to Marty, "Otherwise the next time you go out for cigarettes, walk down to the duck pond, bend over to get the newspaper off the edge of the lawn, we will be gone. Me, the kids, the house itself. One spin around the block and you'll come back to a parking lot, to a quarter acre of potatoes. The neighbors won't even remember what was here."

"Does your brother know you're here?"

"Dead to him," Doe says. "Sat shiva over me, tore his shirt."

"What'd you do?" Marty asks.

"Something bad."

"Must've been if you ended up dead to such a generous man."

A male orderly tries to get them out of their chairs for dinner. He condescends, addresses Doe as a half-wit. Without moving anything but his arm, Doe, with surprising alacrity, reaches out and grabs the orderly's inner thigh. Doe has a good grip, judging by the orderly's whimpering and the number of nurses it takes to pry his fingers free.

"Well, now you've done it," Marty says. And Doe *has* done it; they lock him up in solitary for the rest of the day.

He embarrasses them. That is Marty's great sin. And Robin, whenever she accuses him of it, makes sure he understands exactly how he has transgressed, whether he has embarrassed them into deeper debt, or further embarrassed the family's future. There are also the endless public embarrassments, which consist, as far as he can tell, of Marty's being himself and his loved ones being ashamed.

It is this last form that first landed Marty in the rabbi's study eight years back. A little prank, a tug at a bathing suit, some joking around with Sammy and his friends at the public pool.

The picture frames on the rabbi's desk stand clear in Marty's mind. The rabbi across that broad desktop, and the many black backs of frames, like tombstones, between them.

"My own kid, Rabbi." Marty had been on the defensive. "My own son says to me, 'I wish you were dead.'"

"And so he hits him." Robin with both hands on the purse in her lap, finishing his sentences. "First he mortifies his son, then slaps Sammy so hard he knocks a tooth loose."

"A baby tooth," Marty had said.

"Turned my baby's cheek blue." Robin started crying. She didn't reach for a tissue either, just let her makeup run, hands resting on her bag. "I can't live like this, Rabbi. I'm still a young woman." And the rabbi—how odd now, remembering. The rabbi, Doe's brother, his own hidden shame—he had circled round the desk, had grabbed hold of their chairs and lowered his head.

"Do you think Marty would have been created in this way," the rabbi said, "if he were not also given the means to triumph over his condition? Do you think, Robin, that your husband would have special needs if his wife were not special enough to hold the family together?"

Craning their necks, looking into his face, they both considered the questions. The rabbi smiled a warm clergyman's smile. "This is not about God," he said. "It's not about religion. What this is, is basic humanity. To shirk our responsibilities to each other as human beings is to let the family unit crumble, to hurry society as a whole on its return to dust."

The rabbi stepped back in a half bow, his fingers trailing off the backs of the chairs. Robin reached in her purse and pulled out her car keys, then snapped it closed.

"He turned my Sammy's cheek blue."

"Wishing me dead, my own son." Marty slapped at his chest. "That," he said, "turned my whole life blue."

With Doe locked away Marty turns his chair toward the window; he reads three chapters of his book; he calls home frequently to make sure his family is still there. He hangs up on his wife. He gets information from his daughter. And tries, over and over again, to catch his son.

Sammy answers the phone.

"Hiyah," Marty says. "Heh, there." The boy will have nothing to do with him when he's like this, so Marty strikes quick: "Everything going OK? School OK? Any new girlfriends?"

"You can't be serious." Marty is surprised by his son. Proud. Already a cynical little man.

"Sure I'm serious. I called special to talk to you. You know," Marty says, "you're allowed to come by and visit. What I've got's not catchy, I can promise you that. Like painting a picture or carrying a tune, like people who can bend their thumbs all the way back. You've either got it or you don't. Understand?"

Nothing. Only silence.

"You were born here for Christ's sake. Don't you even want to see the place?"

Sammy hangs up the phone.

These are the things his Leah has told him: The rabbi kept calling as he had promised Marty he would. The rabbi continued to call even after Robin asked him not to—until Robin told him to say she wouldn't take his calls. "Tell Marty that I wouldn't talk to you," her mother had said. "Tell him I slammed down the receiver in your ear." As far as Leah could tell, the rabbi was happy with this. He never called again.

Marty is a Kohen, of the priestly class of Jews. In the Orthodox community in which they live this holds weight. The Levites wash Marty's hands on High Holydays. During the repetition of the Eighteen Benedictions he approaches the ark in stocking feet and drapes his tallis over his head. He fans his fingers, presses together his thumbs, and, turning to face the congregation, blesses them in the name of God.

Out of the one hundred and seven families who attend, there are only eight Kohanim, including Marty and his son. The first aliyah to the Torah, the first called up to say the blessing over the weekly portion, goes to the Kohen. Marty should have been called up for an aliyah every eighth week. He kept a tally in his head. They had cycled three times fully and not once called his name.

Marty knew why they passed over him but considered his community self-righteous and unjust. They shushed him when he sang louder than the hazzan, and hissed when, in the tradition of the Talmudists, he engaged the rabbi in a dialogue during his speech. Others might behave differently, Marty knew. But he'd committed no crime. The disrespect they showed him, in comparison, was indefensible according to Jewish law—a sin greater than murder for which one loses his place in heaven. Marty had learned this himself from the books that the Habad missionaries, milling about outside Penn Station, give away.

So he had gone up on Saturday to get his aliyah, gone up to the bimah even though the gabbai had called Irv Wexler's name. He felt like tradition was on his side. For what other reasons are birthrights given except to be rightfully claimed? Marty beat Irv to the Torah and grabbed hold of the rollers. He told the gabbai, Dave Falk, to cancel Irv Wexler and call his Hebrew name. Dave Falk rolled his eyes and spoke to Marty out of the side of his mouth. "Marty, this ain't the bank. You can't cut in line."

"Call my name," Marty had said, squeezing tighter as if he wanted Falk to say "uncle," as if every twist to the rollers sent him a rush of pain.

Leah was upstairs in the women's section, consigned to the audience. Robin was home making lunch. Sammy had acted, walked briskly to his father's side. "I'm begging you," he said. He gave his father's sleeve a tug. But Marty was making a point. The gabbai wouldn't take back what he said and looked to the rabbi for help. The rabbi, with all those years of private counseling, could not have known more about whom he was dealing with, could not have had better odds at knowing just what to say. This might be the reason the rabbi stayed in his seat; maybe he was trying to figure out the halachic solution, if it was indeed possible to cancel the aliyah of Irv Wexler—a man present, willing, in good standing and good health. As for talking Marty down, he had to know this couldn't be done.

Irv Wexler was not seeking Talmudic remedies. He had grown up in Brooklyn with Dave Falk and Marty and half the congregation. He had a solution of his own. Irv climbed the two stairs and stepped through the opening in the railing that circled the dais. He told Marty to beat it and gave him a shove. That's how the fight broke out. It was like a boxing match at the Garden, all the men in suits surrounding the ring, the women in the blue seats screaming down from above. It wasn't even Marty, but the gabbai, Dave Falk, who knocked the Torah to the floor.

Very strict. They live by the letter of the law. When a Torah hits the ground, is disgraced in such a way, the community must share in a fast of forty days. They split the days among them.

Thinking back, Marty decided he got short shrift. It was Dave who knocked over the Torah. Robin should have turned Dave Falk out of the house, sent *him* to Five Cedars for a rest.

Leah told Marty this also: The rabbi wasn't the only one making calls. Robin had called the rabbi first. She begged him to cancel the fasting. It was torture, her mother said, to have the community fasting in her husband's name. The rabbi, of all people, knew Marty was a sick man. But Rabbi Baum wouldn't ask anything of anyone. Sick man or not.

"I'm not sick," Marty told Leah. "Do I sound sick to you?

It's a matter of levels. My levels are ajar. Not exactly typhoid fever. It's not the black death, after all. It is a number that doesn't match some other number on some chart. A discrepancy. Only a small discrepancy in my blood."

"It's a waste if you're not going to smoke them," Marty says. Doe takes a second puff to show his good faith. After a day in solitary that's all Marty can expect. "Now don't go trying to prove anything," Marty tells him, "we've got it damn good, as long as we have to be in here." Leaning back in his chair, Marty feels his eyelids sliding down over his eyes. "Like heaven," he says. "It's like being in heaven." Marty means this in so many ways. There is the soft light from the windows and the soft white-clad nurses floating in their silent white shoes down the halls. There are the medications that seep like molasses into all the crevices of the mind. After meds at night, who can say, lying back in bed, that it isn't like being cradled in the dense ether of a cloud?

The luggage is piled by the nurses' station. "His brother is my rabbi," Marty is telling them for the thousandth time. "Now isn't that a kick?" Doe is at his side, waiting for a good-bye.

Marty pulls out a gold-plated card case and hands a business card to Doe. He passes a second to Marjorie. "In case he loses that one," Marty says. He gives her a wink, like it's a private joke. To Doe he says, "Come. You'll stay with us when you get out. You've helped me get better in here. Like your brother, more and more. Next it's my turn to get you back on your feet; no more nights on the street. Stay by me," he says. A slap on the back and a nurse buzzes Marty out the door.

. . .

The house is there when Marty pulls up, no potatoes or parking lots, no wrecking crew tearing down walls. It's evening and all the lights are on. There's a dish on the dining room table and a half-full half gallon of milk—still cool. He finds a glass on the kitchen counter with the last sip forgone; a spaghetti pot soaking in the sink. Sammy's room is a mess as usual. Leah has a family photo album open on top of the schoolbooks on her desk. Marty's bedroom, their bedroom, looks as if Robin called in a maid. There is a studied organization to their knickknacks, every surface has a lemony shine. Someone has gathered up all the short, wide, one-hundred-pill bottles of lithium from around the house and piled them into a pyramid in the middle of the dresser. It's something Leah might have done while waiting for her mother. Something her mother might have done instead of saying goodbye.

Marty grabs the pewter ashtray from his night table, takes a fresh pack of cigarettes, and sits down in the middle of the stairs. He pulls at his pant legs and hunkers down, resting his elbows on his knees.

Marty calls the rabbi, sure that Robin would have spoken to him first. "She must have told you something," he says.

"She didn't consult me, Marty. She called me after and didn't leave a number. She said she'd call once a week until you call. And then. Then the usual time, the usual meeting, but not to fix things. In the past I've always talked her into meeting with you when she's given up. Now I'm asking you to give her the same courtesy when, it appears, she's given up for good. She wants to meet you, with me here. To settle things, as it were."

Marty does not tell the rabbi about Doe.

"You should know, Rabbi," he says, "I feel pretty bad about the Torah, even if it was David Falk who knocked it over. I feel bad about messing up the service. I wasn't exactly myself. I hope you understand."

"Things like that shouldn't ever happen, Marty."

"I know, Rabbi. You know I know."

"Yes," the rabbi tells him. "I guess I understand."

"Well, the house is still here. That's a sort of triumph, of sorts." Marty is showing Doe around. The upright piano in the living room. "A gift for my Leah." An antique clock on the mantel: porcelain, fine, detailed with lavender flowers and emitting a slow and masculine tick. "My grandmother brought it from Vienna. Martin, you know, is an Austrian name."

Doe still has his bag in one hand and a paper sack from the Five Cedars pharmacy in the other. Marty has not invited him to put anything down. "They're gone, huh?"

"So it seems," Marty says, "so it seems. Want to see the upstairs?"

"Yeah," Doe says. "Let's."

Marty stops with Doe at each of the doors, following them along the hall. First the master bedroom, spotless, only the pyramid of bottles out of place, then the bathroom, then Leah's room, exactly as it was when he arrived, just as the plate and the glass and the now sour carton of milk sit out downstairs. "Sammy's room," Marty says at the end of the hallway. "You can stay in here." Marty considers his friend for the first time since his arrival, as if giving him the once-over for a menial job. Doe is clean shaven. His jeans and shirt, dingy but laundered. His old boots, shined up.

The room is a mess.

"Like a museum," Doe says. "The ones with the rooms that you can't go in. Rooms with glass half filling the doors."

"I can see that," Marty says. "Very sharp. They sharpened you right up in there." Marty enters first, feigning ease. "Make yourself at home. But don't touch anything. When they come back I want it all right as it was." Marty lifts a record album from the unmade bed. A sock hangs by its heel from the record's sleeve. He puts it on the desk across the room.

"What's with the sock?" Doe says.

"Tape," Marty tells him. "It has to be just right."

They both nap. Marty in Leah's and Doe in Sammy's bed. Marty is up first and walks down the hall, comforted to see someone sleeping under the covers. "Wake up," he says, and gives Doe a shake. He looks at his watch. It's time for them to take their pills.

"What?" Doe says. "Sleep," he says.

"I told you," Marty tells him. "I'm going to get your life on track this time. That means schedules—for both of us. Dinner at dinnertime. Sleeping at night. Awake during the day." Doe has lined his pill bottles up on the base of the night-table lamp. Marty goes through the prescriptions as Doe stirs.

There is one name that he doesn't recognize. A pill he has not taken or read about or heard mention of before. He pops the cap and pours a couple of giant green tablets into his hand.

"What the hell are these horse pills for?"

"Which?" Doe says, his eyes still closed.

"Green. And dry looking."

"They're supposed to keep me from turning violent."

"Do they work?"

"Never have before."

The owner of the kosher pizza place is a member of Ohav Shalom. She is a kind woman and keeps a tab for Marty. She knows Robin will eventually take care of the bills. She always does.

Marty and Doe share a table for four. Marty is in a suit and wears a black yarmulke, Doe is wearing a yarmulke of Sammy's, the boy's name knit around the border by a girl in his class. Doe looks like a bum even clean. The customers stare without restraint.

Marty and Doe eat an extra-large pizza. They drink can after can of Dr. Brown's black cherry soda.

Doe is a grand listener, even off the ward. Marty has never had someone with the same background and similar problems to talk with before. He has never been open in the down-there world, never been honest off the ward. Now he sits out in public talking, telling Doe about his first episode as if it were first love.

"There is nothing in your body then. No inhibitors, no drugs. And it all happens at once. The response is hidden somewhere in your makeup, building up for a lifetime, waiting with its own biology, its own need to be born. For me, it started with synesthesia. I'm outside walking and it's a bright day. Summer. And I can see the grass. And it's green. And I can smell the grass but it's not grass smell, it's green smell. And I can taste it and hear it and everything, my whole me was green-grass green. It lasted a minute or a second or an hour. But I saw what I could do. What I could make happen. Like when you wake up in a dream and know it's a dream and until you fall out of it you can fly and fuck strangers and turn yourself into an astronaut or a wolf. But I was calm, and feeling good, and thinking about my dead mother. I loved her so much. Missed her like anything. And so that's what I used it for. And she was there in this all-around all-sense way, and I could talk to her and touch her and remember her while I walked with her. See her young and old in the same blink of an eye. It was a miracle. And I walked in that miracle for a day and a night and a day. And I brought my mother home that way, the whole experience of her. I was so happy, so overjoyed and overwhelmed and at peace, I wanted to show Robin. To have Robin see this, to share this all-sensory, all-being, honest-to-goodness miracle with my wife."

"She couldn't," Doe says.

"Of course not. I didn't even get to explain it. A whole mess. She was outside dragging me into the house soon as I turned the corner. She was crying, shrieking: Where had I been and where were my shoes and how did I cut my leg and how in the hell could I laugh? Well, how could she scream in the face of the magic of that moment? She just went on with her tantrum. The kids, small, were terrified. Right to the hospital. Right then. And I lost it on the way. The ability. I didn't get to say goodbye. And I wanted to, desperately. A chance to say it right, no one gets that. I had it and I wanted it. And I tried for it in the car. I was clawing at this all-around place, trying to get back in." Marty leans over, takes hold of Doe's arm. "I never admitted to anything. Knew enough to deny it. But that feeling, that last time with my mother, it's as real to me as my wedding day. Only it's more real because it was better than real. More wonderful and amazing than anything I've experienced before or since. And sometimes it's too tempting to try to get there again. To skip the meds and see where I land. Now tell me—how am I supposed to explain that to Robin?"

"Can't," Doe says.

"Exactly. That's why I need your brother. He gets her back for me. He swings things my way with Jewish family talk and pity-for-the-ill and lots-in-life and fathers-for-children. He talks her home for me."

"Does he know that I'm with you?"

"No," Marty says. "But he'll find out on Wednesday. Robin wants to see me at his house. We'll have a double reunion. You and I will arrive all gussied up and well balanced. They will look at us and know. It will be emotional—that can't be helped. People will cry. Maybe all of us. But they will see us looking handsome and healthy, and your brother, the master of forgiveness, will be first. His usual fine example. And then both families will be reunited. Simple as that."

There was finagling involved, a call for the manager, some trained, disgruntled-customer-style indignation, and Marty succeeded in getting his Brooks Brothers account reinstated. Both he and Doe left for the reunion at Rabbi Baum's house in sharp, classic pinstripes—the picture of sober style.

Doe fiddles with the glove compartment. He tries to slide his hand into a jacket pocket sewn shut.

"Probably I should wait," he says.

Marty turns off the main avenue onto Baum's block. He stops the car.

"No, sir. We should go in there together. Dazzle them. Sweep them off their feet with our fine appearance and good intentions."

"Tell him first," Doe says. "Go tell him that I'm here."

"And what, you'll sit in the car and wait? Like an idiot?"

"Yes," Doe says, "an idiot."

"Won't have it. We'll make our entrance together. A pair of fallen men reborn."

Robin is talking to the rebbetsen on the front steps as Marty and Doe make their way up the slate walk.

"Moish," the rebbetsen calls into the house. "Moish, get out here," she calls through the closed storm door. It is the tone she uses when the children fall and there is blood. Robin turns and her smile drops away. Rabbi Baum is out on the steps, his breathing short. He does not touch his wife in public, and over the years physical cues have been shunted into looks. He gives his; she responds. Wordless. And he focuses on the man behind Marty.

A reunion. The rabbi runs down the stairs. He is a small man, narrow, though his face is large, with the tacked-up eyes. A Baum face, if ever there was. As he approaches, Marty thinks he may be reversing in scale, getting smaller instead of larger with every step.

"A nightmare," Rabbi Baum says. "Horrible enough over the years, wondering when you'd be in together. Each time you were out, I'd wait, then nothing. I thought maybe I'd be spared."

"Your brother, Rabbi. Looking like a million bucks."

The rebbetsen covers her mouth with both hands. She is talking, you can tell, into her palms. Robin makes her way over.

"Who is this?" she yells. "Tell me what you've done."

The rabbi and Doe stand staring at each other. The similarities between them are clear.

"The rabbi's brother, Robin. He was in with me on the ward. A fluke. A friendship. He sleeps in Sammy's bed. Today is the day of the double reunion. I've brought the rabbi's brother back from the dead."

The rabbi takes his brother by the shoulders. He does not hug him but turns him around. "Go," he says, "back to your gutter. Take your fancy clothes and get away."

"No reunions," Robin says. "No more wasted life."

"Go," the rabbi yells. He stamps a foot, as one might to scare off a cat. Doe is still facing the street, his cheeks and neck and ears turning bright red.

"Take it easy there," Marty says and touches Doe's arm. "We don't want any trouble." Marty says this to all of them. "We are better now, under control. We have made mistakes and now we are sorry."

"You are a man without boundaries," the rabbi tells Marty. "There are limits, prescribed, written. You've overshot, both of you. Mercy is not required. Nowhere does it say I must forgive." From behind the rebbetsen's hands comes a noise, a weird triple-sound that is yelling and crying and praying to God. And behind her, in window after window, faces begin to pop up. One little one behind the storm door tries to get out. The rebbetsen steps in front of her, stands half in and half out of the house, watching from behind the glass of the door.

Marty does not answer. He is watching the rebbetsen and the half-open door. He can't help but think of that sweet stink from their house, the by-product of life, of their happy home, seeping out into the air. Seal it in, he wants to tell her. If they ever leave, you will need it to survive.

"Go, both of you get away." The rabbi shoves his brother in the back, and Doe takes a baby step forward.

"But you haven't made peace yet," Marty tells him. "Your job. My rabbi. The fate of the Jewish family. Look at how my wife hates me for no reason. She hasn't agreed to come home."

"No more forgiveness," she says. "Nothing left in me for anyone's sake."

"I'm out of advice," the rabbi says, such a pale little man, trying to sound as if he has some control. "Maybe it's better if your family goes broken. Sometimes, in extreme cases, there is nothing more to be done."

"There's always more," Doe says. Turns back. "Even brothers beyond forgiveness surface looking for more. Even knowing what they've done."

"You'll go!" The rabbi again tries to turn him, but this time Doe does not give. He takes his brother's hands from his shoulders, pushes him back and away. Rabbi Baum catches a heel, hitches a foot on a piece of slate. He trips. He falls to the ground, bounces, and rocks his head.

"You will be the same until the end of time," Robin says. "You will torture us all and live long past when we're dead. A sick man is not a devil. You, Marty, are both." She spits at his feet and curses him.

But it was Doe that knocked the rabbi down, not Marty. He feels that she should curse Doe. Spit at *his* feet. This would be more fair, after all.

The rebbetsen runs down to her husband. Robin moves over to the rabbi but does not bend or ask if he's hurt. Doe stands, red faced, his hands balled into fists. And Marty looks up at all the many faces of the children filling the windows and wonders, If forty days are accorded a Torah, how long must a child fast when his father is knocked to the ground?

The Wig

Colors and styles, she takes note of. Hemlines, accessories, heel width and height. Also, that the girls get taller every month, bonier and more sickly looking. Ruchama had quite a figure herself as a girl, kept it until the first three children were born. But never, from the age of twelve, was she without a chest and a bottom. She really can't imagine how these fence posts manage to sit down.

It's hair that Ruchama is studying. She goes through the new *Bazaar* page by page. The magazines are contraband in Royal Hills, narishkeit, vain and immodest, practically pornographic. But she needs to keep up. Her customers will bring her pictures like these, folded up small and stuck into wallets, bra cups, pulled from under the wigs they wear. And they expect Ruchama to be familiar. They are relieved when she takes a wrinkled photo, nods with confidence, and says, "Yes, again they are highlighting bangs."

Ruchama has come into the city for the silk caps onto which she and Tzippy—best friend and right hand—knot the hair. The newsstand is at Twenty-third and Sixth, convenient to her supplier and far enough from Royal Hills, oddly enough located, that she will not see anyone she knows. She flips through the magazines between Jamal's stand and the trash basket on the corner. She pays for her browsing rights, forces Jamal to accept the crumpled bill she drops on the counter when new issues arrive. She thinks this appropriate. For she would take them home if she could and knows that, if a familiar face appears in the crowd, she'll drop the magazines in the basket and fall in with the flow of foot traffic, crossing whichever way the walk sign allows.

She does not spot anyone. She finishes flipping through the magazines. She places them, one by one, back in their slots on the rack. Good as new.

Tzippy carries a box of braids down the inside stairs to the workshop.

"New hair," she says, and drops the UPS package on the separating table.

Ruchama spits three times to ward off the evil eye. Whenever a box of braids arrives from Eastern Europe there is always a shadow, a gloomy revenant. Tzippy drinks her tea. Ruchama pinches the flat of a double-edged razor blade between her fingers and with three quick passes sets the tape on the box whistling and folds open the cardboard flaps.

Taking out a braid, Ruchama pulls her thumb across a blunt end, letting the tips fan back with natural spring. Like a paintbrush. Good and thick. She holds it up to the light, checking color. She and Tzippy never refer to colors by their useless names. They have learned from disappointments, stood united before a red, red wig they had spent two months creating while a client screamed at them, literally screamed, "Does that look red to you?" They had squinted, moved closer, adjusted lamps. What else was it but red? They have learned. There are over one million shades of auburn, two million meanings for "chestnut brown." They now work in similes: "Darker or lighter than pumpernickel bread?" "Newsprint black? Or black like black beetles in black ink?"

Judging the braid she holds, Ruchama places it in one corner of the vast separating table. From there they will build outward, creating a map of color and length and curl.

Tzippy puts down her tea and reaches into the box. "Wet wood spoons," she says, displaying her choice. That is exactly the color. Ruchama is always amazed by her accuracy.

Tzippy begins unraveling the braid, brushing through the hair with her fingers and burying her face in it. She is smelling for a past, sniffing out the woman's shampoo and sweat, the staleness of cigarettes or the smoke that drifts down from some factory nearby. She breathes deep. She is onto a scent, a wind from a village, a mist of perfume.

"They are paid top dollar," Ruchama tells her.

"Women with choices leave their hair to be swept off salon floors," Tzippy says.

"Maybe these women are more prudent."

"With such hair?" Tzippy waves the braid's open end at Ruchama. "These are women who have to sell some part of themselves and this is where they begin. This one," she says, sniffing again, "is on break at a bottling plant thinking of her lover. She sold her hair to pay his gambling debts and she wonders now where her hair is and where that bum has gone."

"My own life is depressing enough, Tzippy. Why must you make it like we're scalping orphans?"

"A teenage girl," Tzippy says, "a girl with everything she needs. Only, there is a used scooter her parents won't buy her and a boyfriend she lusts after who lives all the way on the other side of the lake."

"You've been reading novels again, Tzippy. Don't tell me there isn't a romance hidden under your bed."

The front room gets natural light from the windows that open onto the cellar well. The room is carpeted and painted and, in front of the long windows, there is a pair of comfortable chairs. There are stools and a counter, and on the counter mirrors—one standing on a silverplate base and an assortment of hand mirrors that Ruchama has no real attachment to, though it is intended to appear to customers that she does.

Ruchama finds it difficult to live up to the expectations of the room. She is more comfortable in the back with Tzippy on the cement, hair-strewn floor of the work space.

Nava Klein is sitting on an overstuffed chair in front of the window. Tzippy sits on a stool, her feet resting on the crossbar. Ruchama stands; she looks better standing, her dress hanging loose off her chest, concealing. She has not sat down in front of Nava Klein in at least half-a-dozen years.

The whole back wall is covered with framed photographs of wigs on Styrofoam heads. Nava is pointing to one. "Third in," she says. "That's got to be Aviva Sussman." Ruchama's work is so distinct, you can pick out half the neighborhood.

"You can't tell me that's not Aviva's hair."

"Please," Tzippy says.

Nava grimaces, turns her attention to Ruchama.

"I saw your oldest," she says. "A real beauty and such a rail. She reminds me of you when you were that age. You were striking, striking as a girl." Nava sighs, signals with her head to Tzippy, as if she were not part of the adult conversation. "Only Tzippy stays the same, her hipbones pushing at the front of her skirt. The rest of us ragged old women have to hide behind our daughters' good looks."

Nava shakes her head. "How do you do it, Tzippy? Where in Brooklyn is your fountain of youth?"

Tzippy blushes. Ruchama wants to scream. Every compliment the woman gives releases a dandelion's worth of barbed spores. Tzippy looks great because she is barren. Her figure has been spared because her womb has walls of stone. And Ruchama, she is a proud mother. Of course she is, with six wonderful children and a chin to show for each one.

"I've an appointment a week from Thursday with Kendo of Kendo Keller's," Nava says. "He is going to advise me. And then, of course, he'll style the wig. It's not you, Tzippy. You're a natural. A brilliant stylist. The best of the sheitel machers. But this isn't exactly Madison Avenue. It's only that I want a more contemporary look this year. So vain."

In the mirror that night, Ruchama takes her face off, rubbing hard, removing makeup, working at the base that catches like grit in the folds of her skin.

She used to be the prettiest, prettier than Tzippy and Nava. They all three used to play together in Tzippy's room. They tried on clothes and dreamed of marriages—to brilliant scholars flown in from Jerusalem, handsome princes who would sit in the back of deep studies while Jews the world over came to their doors begging wisdom, advice, a blessing in exchange for a kiss on the hand.

They do come from around the world. But not for Shlomi, not for her husband. They circle the globe to see Ruchama, because they are trapped in their modesty and want to feel, even as illusion, the simple pleasure of wind in their hair.

Menucha, the littlest, is splashing in the tub next to Ruchama. Ruchama begs quiet when Menucha squeals. She quizzes the child on body parts while taking off her makeup, testing to see where the girl has and has not scrubbed. "Ears?" she says. "Elbows? Belly button. Toes."

Shlomi is home from the study hall making noise in the kitchen. Cabinets slam. A pot hits a countertop, a pan strikes a burner. The new rules of her home. Six children, and for the first time all are out of the house during the day. Menucha in first grade and Shira, the oldest, in tenth. For once Ruchama can work uninterrupted, and her taste for independence has spread. She has instituted small chores for Shlomi. She asks now that he heat his own dinner and wash his own dishes, as well as the stray glasses and spoons that accumulate between the children's dinner and bed. Over this he makes a production.

To take off her makeup slowly, to look in the mirror and be sad, that's all she wants. Shlomi calls out questions, makes comments to reiterate his helplessness. "Where is the dairy sponge?" "This soap is no good!" Ruchama doesn't respond, does not care where the soap falls short in his eyes. He trayfs up her kitchen to spite her. He is forever putting meat silverware in the dairy sink.

He calls up: "Are there any dry dish towels?"

She screams so that Menucha stops splashing, her little arms frozen in the air. Ruchama screams with murder in her voice, her own hand checked in midmotion, a dollop of face cream on the pads of her fingers. "Reach down," she yells, "pull open the towel drawer, and look." She spreads the cream under her eyes. It is nice and cool. "When the drawer is open," she screams, "bend over and open your eyes."

She waits for him to ask where, in their house of sixteen years, is the dry-dish-towel drawer.

When Louise arrives there are kisses and hugs. She peels off her gloves, undoes a silk scarf with a pull. Tzippy and Ruchama have a crush on her. She is their only secular client, the only one to traipse down the stairs in plunging necklines and smart man-tailored slacks. She reminds Ruchama of the pretty ladies who stand in department stores spraying perfume.

Louise has a daughter their age, yet, Ruchama thinks, she looks younger than Nava. It is only the thick, tired veins on the backs of her hands and the carefully organized hairline that give her away. Louise takes Ruchama's arm and kisses her again.

"I've done it," Louise says. "You'll both be furious, but don't feel bad. I couldn't tell my husband—not about the wig and not about the money." Louise unzips her pocketbook.

"Our thirtieth anniversary. My present from Harold. A stunning necklace he picked out himself. Pawned. I sold it away."

"You didn't," Tzippy says. Her expression is embarrassingly happy. She is a fan of intrigue.

"I did," Louise says. "A purchase must be paid for."

"Credit," Ruchama says dryly. "I offered you credit."

"I know, dear. But it's not right. I went and pawned it and told Harold that the clasp broke and that I had put the floater on my to-do list but hadn't let the insurance man know. 'Off premises' doesn't cover it, and Harold would never fake a claim." She takes an envelope from her purse and extends her arm with impelling force. "Here," she says, passing off the envelope, thick with fifties, to Ruchama.

When she made her first appearance she had, in the same businesslike fashion, pulled a different envelope from her purse. "You must be Ruchama," she had said. "These are pictures of me when my hair was as it should be. I want my wig like that, but better." Ruchama had fallen in love with her right then. A woman who can present an envelope with such confidence can get anything done in this world. "My daughter says you are the best and the most expensive. That's what I want. No bargains. I want it to feel so horribly overpriced that I'll be convinced it's good." Then Louise struck a pose in those smart slacks—one knee locked, the other bent, one foot straight, the other pointing out—exactly as Ruchama would have liked to if she were permitted such a thing. "If my daughter hasn't told you, I'm being attacked by menopause and it's taking my hair, and both my doctors admit I am, in reality, going bald. Give me whatever you've got, I told them. If it kills me, that's fine. I'll take six gorgeous months over one hundred years of what's in store." She had then presented a locket. Pried it open. There was a curl pressed inside. "My baby hair. Russet. Virginal and fine. Match it. That is the color of my wig."

And now, months later, Ruchama locks the money in the

strongbox and locks the strongbox in her desk. She takes out the pictures and the locket and goes over to the cubbies. She takes down Louise's wig on its Styrofoam base. It is majestic. She brings it out and Louise presses her hands to her head.

"Oh, yes," she says. "That is me." She messes up her own hair, so carefully sprayed in place. "This is not me, that is. You've got it there. Now give it up."

They seat Louise on a stool and fit the wig on her head. She leans in to the standing mirror. Ruchama and Tzippy hover behind, hand mirrors poised. Louise does, truly, they all agree, look spectacular. She spreads the old photos out on the counter. She goes back and forth between the mirror and the pictures. She opens the locket. "Russet," she says. She puts it around her neck and turns to face the women.

"Goddesses," she says. "Miracle workers. I feel like I have my life back, my youth. I'm nineteen years old again," she says. "And I am beautiful."

The new issues are at least two weeks away, but there are things Ruchama wants to double-check, an idea or two that she has. She takes the magazines off the rack with a nod.

"Sold your copies," Jamal says. He is on the same side of the stand, stocking mints and chocolate bars where they are low. "Same issue, different copies."

"I'll pay again, if that's what you're getting at."

She reaches for her purse.

"Teasing," he says. "Help yourself. No camp for the kids this summer, is all."

They used to dream of being fashion models, Tzippy and Nava and Ruchama. They had plans. They would take only modest jobs, stroll down the runways with floor-length skirts and high-collared shirts, sleeves that buttoned at the wrists. They would be sensations. They walked the length of Tzippy's room, spinning in front of her full-length mirror, spotting their heads to catch themselves in the turn.

She finds the advertisement, the one she was thinking of, a woman turning in a New York street, her hair in an arc, banana curls, full and light.

She presses the magazine down on the counter. She presses a finger to the page. Jamal looks.

"That's what my hair was like," she says, "when I was a girl."

"Hmmm," he says, "nice." He folds an empty carton. Stops to rub his hands together, blows into them against the cold. "Looks nice now," he says, "plenty nice."

Ruchama goes red. This is what familiarity breeds.

"A wig," she says to Jamal. "I'm wearing a wig."

"I'll tell you," he says, "looks for real. I wondered, too. You dress Jewish and I wondered. All the other Hasid ladies wear wigs and scarves and such. And I'd wondered what's with you."

"Human hair," she says. She is proud. "A good-quality wig and you should never be able to tell. They wear poor quality, the others. Acrylic fibers. Junk stuff. Wigs made from recycled cola bottles and used plastic bags."

The advertisement stays with Ruchama: this young woman spinning in a New York street. It's an ad for shampoo. The woman has caused a traffic jam by half raising her finger for a taxi. Everyone is watching her from the sidewalk. She is smiling and so is all of New York. Even the cabdrivers—white and handsome, all with a slight scruff—are smiling. They laugh as they lock fenders trying to give this woman with the long, lovely hair a ride.

Ruchama wants to feel sexy like that, to chuckle at the bedlam her beauty causes. How nice it would be to arrive at shul looking trim and with the long, beautiful hair of her youth, to see Nava's eyes widen and for the men to stand on tiptoes trying to peek into the women's section and for the rabbi to stamp a foot and the gabbai to slap the bimah, for people to hiss for quiet as she takes her seat. She'd have her oldest save one right in front of Nava. All would whisper. Is that mother or sister? they would want to know.

Shlomi will be home late. It is his night to help clean at the yeshiva. There he can push a broom. She decides to put on her sexy skirt and wait up. It's formfitting but not wholly immodest; it falls, just barely, on the permissible side of the line. She puts it on but cannot close the button—does not get the zipper high enough along to try. She throws it into the back of her closet. She tiptoes to the bathroom, all the children asleep. She touches up her makeup and puts on a nightgown; she gets under the covers and pretends to sleep. She leaves the lamp on next to Shlomi's bed. Ruchama does not say her prayers.

Shlomi comes into the room and makes an attempt at quiet. At the first noise, the jiggling of keys being removed from a pocket, Ruchama sighs and throws down her blanket as if waking.

She tries hard to be enticing. Shlomi is not having it. When he gets into his bed she reaches over and strokes the inside of his arm. He takes her hand, squeezes it. "Good night," he says, and switches off the light.

That he's not interested is fine.

That she's not interested is what she is burning to tell him. She'd rather pull the man who delivers groceries upstairs, all muscular and sweaty in his hard-work way. She'd rather have sex with him and scream out loud instead of worrying with every breath that she'll wake the children along the hall.

She turns to her side. She puts a hand between her thighs and presses the one hand with the other, squeezing her thighs together and rocking herself. The half of her thoughts connected to Shlomi and anger and the skirt in her closet she forgets, focusing on the grocery-boy and the cabdriver models and fingers in her hair. She is alone with her thoughts, rocking.

Shlomi switches his light on. He shakes her shoulder, speeding up her rhythm, interrupting.

"Ruchie, you promised."

"I did no such thing."

"Either way, it must stop. It's an abomination."

"Where is it written? For a man, yes. For a woman—seedless as a supermarket grape—it's fine. Go ask your rebbe. He'll tell you. Tell him what your wife does and ask if it's allowed."

"Ask him? God forbid."

"You should have been Christian," she says. "An expert at avoiding earthly pleasures."

"God forbid. How you talk!" She turns to see that he has clasped his hands to his ears like a child. She clasps her hands deeper into her crotch. All of his passion trapped between those ears, she thinks, and rocks and rocks and rocks herself to sleep.

"You have zero choice in the matter. She's out there waiting. She's talking about four wigs by Pesach. We're talking about twenty thousand dollars."

"I can't do it, Tzippy." Ruchama is sitting at her desk, going over some accounting. "I can't face Nava now. I'm too weak for her compliments. She'll praise me into the grave today. I'm telling you."

"I told her you were on the phone to Israel."

"Tell her I went to the city. I'll go for real. I have errands."

"You were just in the city yesterday."

"So? It's so out of the ordinary? People don't go in every morning? The subway driver doesn't cross the river ten times in a day?"

Nava is in the deep chair by the window. She is wearing an Armani suit tailored to the knee. Too short, by far. She has new boots on and a new bag rests on the floor. Ruchama keeps her eyes moving, doesn't lag over a single item to avoid giving Nava satisfaction.

"I was telling Tzippy—" Nava says, pauses. "Any news from Israel?"

"No," Ruchama says. "Raining in Jerusalem," she says.

Nava shifts, moves the new bag onto her lap. Ruchama looks out the window.

"I was telling Tzippy, Kendo is an absolute genius. Part hair designer, part philosopher. 'Tell me about the best hair,' he said. 'Talk.' And you know what I told him, Ruchama? I told him about your wedding day. I told him how you were the first to marry and how you had the most perfect hair, how it made you who you were, a girl and a woman, religious and wild. And then I told him how you cut it off for your wedding. I cried mixed tears at your bedekken. Here was the miracle of marriage and the sadness of your lost hair. You were so beautiful before. A perfect-looking thing."

"Thank you," Ruchama says. She moves to the chair next to Nava's and drops deep into the seat.

"So we follow this trail," Nava says, leaning forward. "We go off in search of the ideal me. And we find her. And she has long hair. That is where the true me lies. Of course, I can't just appear with long hair. It's immodest enough to start with. But to shock people on top of it is inconceivable. 'Not a problem,' he says. A genius. 'Four wigs,' he says. 'The same hair, the same color. Only different lengths. We will mock the natural process of growth. Wig by wig.' That's his plan. 'Slowly,' he says, 'naturally. Wig by wig, reclaiming freedom.'"

Nava leaves. Ruchama is still splayed in the chair. Melted.

"I'm sorry," Tzippy says. "Go to the city now. I'll finish the list for today."

"That's OK."

"You go," Tzippy says. "It'll do you good."

. . .

The streets fill up with evening traffic. Jamal exits the kiosk and puts on a surplus pea coat. Ruchama is at the corner flipping through the magazines.

"Night guy's here," Jamal says. He buttons his coat. "Have a good one."

"You too," Ruchama says.

"New issues come tomorrow. Next day at the latest."

"I'll make an effort," she says. Their conversation is split by the rattle and clatter of a dolly as it fails and then manages to make its way onto the curb. There is a potted tree on the dolly, and the tree seems to lunge at one and then the other of them, directed by a reckless driver and undirected by a clattery and wandering wheel. "Fucking tree," the driver says as he passes. Ruchama follows him, takes a step and then two. She is mesmerized.

He has, unconditionally, the most beautiful hair she's ever seen. Completely tamed, completely full. He has a mane of curls the color of toasted bamboo that runs down to the middle of his back and ends in a deep, blunt ridge. The curls are singular, full and moist, and they stack well. A head of hair with personality. She is obsessed, she knows. But the obsession is not what makes his hair beautiful; it is the obsession that makes her take notice of hair when she has nearly been bowled over by an amuck and wayward tree.

"That's the kind of hair," Ruchama says to Jamal, pointing.

"Damn nice," Jamal says. "Make a hell of a wig, I'd bet."

"It would make a half dozen," Ruchama says. She keeps an eye on the tree as it darts back and forth above the crowd. "I have a room where clients wait. Two big chairs in front of two tall windows. No views." She hands the magazines to Jamal. "A tree might look nice in between."

Ruchama follows him to a jungle on Twenty-eighth Street, where the tree disappears into a storefront thick with tropical foliage. There is a path down the middle. Ruchama steps in, and a pair of birds start from a bush and fly toward an empty cage. The man works the tree off the dolly with a thud.

"Nice tree."

"Return," he says. "Designer lady wanted an orange tree for the lobby. Says I didn't tell her it won't have oranges until summer." The man wears a metal stud through his chin. It moves up and down when he speaks, freezes when he doesn't—like permanent punctuation. A stainless-steel period under his lip. "No such thing as a used tree," he says, "but I'll give you a deal on it if you want."

"Are you here in the morning?"

"Every morning."

"I'll be back tomorrow with cash."

A homeless man begs a dollar as Ruchama climbs out of the subway on Twenty-third. She usually gives, always gives, but she has all her deposits with her, including Louise's envelope with four thousand dollars in cash. Morning rush hour has barely started; it's not the time to open her purse in the street. She clutches her bag, moving on toward the newsstand. "That's OK," the homeless man yells after her. "I forgive you because you pregnant."

The magazines are up against the stand, tied in bales. Jamal pushes a box cutter toward her, and she pushes a crumpled twenty-dollar bill his way.

"You do the honors," he says. Ruchama rubs a hand to her face; she still has sleep in her eyes.

It's unseasonably warm and cloudless. Ruchama sits on the

sidewalk like the homeless man and leans her back against the newsstand. She is looking for her advertisement. She crosses her ankles, turns her face to the sun. It's been ten years, twenty, since she's sat on the ground.

The shampoo girl is there right after the contents page. She has been bobbing for apples at the state fair. She has failed to snatch an apple with her delicate mouth. She is pulling her head from the barrel, and her drenched hair follows, caught in an arc above. A rainbow streaks the glimmering hair and the splash of water that will rain on the gathered crowd. Everyone is smiling. The carny in the booth is handing the woman a teddy bear anyhow. All the other carnies in the surrounding booths are also reaching out with prizes. They are all white men, handsome, with a slight scruff. One, she remembers, was driving a cab.

Ruchama looks off down Sixth Avenue and loses herself in the traffic moving toward her. It is the coming Passover and she has the long hair of her childhood. Everyone is out in front of shul, talking, making lunch plans on the front stoop. Nava is there in a gaudy creation; she is wearing the first of her new wigs. A car will race by, souped up like a gangster's, and the young handsome man in the passenger seat, a strong arm hanging out the window, will whistle in a lewd manner. Ruchama, startled, will blush and spin, her hair opening up in the turn like a peacock's fan.

"I sell plants and bushes and trees. I sell peat and mineral-enriched soils. For one hundred dollars you can have a dozen calathea. I will do you a deal on orchids."

"You have your earrings and your tattoos," Ruchama tells the plant man. "You have nice features and are tall and slim. You have plenty to make them look. You don't need the hair."

"I've had it forever," he says. "It's defining."

"Of course it is. Do you think I do this every day? From Eastern Europe; from Poland; that's where I get my hair. Never from the street. If not for one hundred dollars, how much is not-for-sale hair worth?"

"You know," he says, "I'm thinking you're a freak."

"Yes," Ruchama says, "we are both freaks, you and I. It is only that we are different in different ways. So tell me. Two hundred dollars, five hundred dollars?"

"One thousand dollars, two thousand dollars. It doesn't matter. I'm not selling."

"I have four thousand dollars here," she says. "In cash. You can have it all."

And then, with finesse, with Louise in her mind's eye, she pulls the envelope out of her purse and sticks it in his hand. "I have brought my own scissors, you only need to sit down."

"Damn," he says, counting. "Why don't I just keep it? Why don't I just pretend I never saw you and keep the money and the hair?"

"Because it's America," Ruchama says. "You will sell me your hair, you will deliver the tree, and if you keep the money I will bring the police and you will give it back. That is the wonder of this country. Jews have rights; women have rights. Maybe you will keep the money anyway, as a challenge. And maybe when the police come, I will tell them you took five thousand, not four. And they will believe me because I have no hole in my lip and because five is a more logical number."

Ruchama pulls out the scissors like a threat. He looks at her and pockets the envelope. Ruchama searches the jungle for a chair.

When the tree arrives, Ruchama locks the door of the work-room with Tzippy out on the other side. She told Tzippy about the tree, an extravagant and spontaneous purchase. She lied to her about the bank deposit and is not sure from where the money to replace it will come.

Tzippy bangs on the door.

"He wants to know where to put it."

Ruchama screams through, "He knows, and you know: between the two chairs." Ruchama is dizzy. She told Tzippy that she is locking the door because of a spate of robberies, deliverymen scouting out the businesses they deliver to and stealing everything inside. She told Tzippy that she met a lady photographer at the supply store who had her whole studio cleaned out by the bike messenger who picked up the film. She had let him linger and drink water from the cooler.

"He wants an extra two hundred dollars, Ruchama." Tzippy is knocking again. "He says you promised him an extra two hundred dollars for delivering the tree."

"No such thing was promised."

"Ruchama, you open this door."

"Give him a hundred and tell him to go away."

"Open this door."

"Give him the hundred and then he will go."

How she has come to love the nights. The minute the last child sleeps, she is down in the basement. The nights used to be so long, and now she sees they are as short as the days.

Without Tzippy there gossiping she gets real work done. She takes over the separating table, laying out the hair, curl by curl. She knots like a demon. It has been aeons since Ruchama made herself a wig. Lately she's been going around in the irregulars with their bald spots and cowlicks, sporting the flawed models they cannot sell.

The year is crowded with holidays. Passover is already bearing down. This keeps her from napping, from wasting time with sleep. When she cut his hair, she secured and then numbered each of the curls separately, like the bricks of a museum-bound temple. This way she could reconstruct them just so. To be perfect, hair must sit just right around the head.

They have nothing to show Nava. They have fallen behind. Ruchama is half mortified and half happy. She would like to fall further behind, leave Nava wigless, forced to show up at shul on the holidays with a bathing cap stretched over her head.

Ruchama moves out front. Tzippy follows with a tray of cookies and tea. Nava is fiddling with the leaves of the orange tree, careful of her nails. She snaps off a leaf.

"It does wonders," she says. "I never told you, but this room was always so depressing. Still. If it's an orange tree, where are the oranges?"

"Not until summer," Ruchama says. "Tricky indoors."

"Shouldn't there be little green marbles or something? With an orange tree you sort of expect—"

"Yes," Ruchama says, "you do. About expecting, I owe you an apology. The hair is late. There is nothing yet to show."

"Ruchie, it's been weeks." Nava bends the leaf in half, snaps a crisp seam down the center.

"We've been crazy," Ruchama says. "We're overwhelmed." Tzippy dips a cookie into her tea.

"I've a right to be mad," Nava says. She faces Ruchama, reaches out, and rests a hand on Ruchama's hip. "But—and you know I only have compliments for you, only compliments—but it shows on your face, Ruchie. You look terrible. You're running yourself into the ground, and I don't want to be the reason. It's not too late to take my order elsewhere if you'd feel better about it. Kendo Keller has a man."

Ruchama *would* feel better about it. "Maybe you should," she says.

"Ruchama!" Tzippy bursts out only with her name. Ruchama understands. There is their reputation. There is the money. And, open wide before her, is all that freed-up time.

"Maybe you should," Ruchama says. "You've always been so understanding."

Tzippy has taken to watching from a distance. She no longer stands at Ruchama's desk with her tea or leans over her shoulder at her worktable. She holds her mug with two hands now and sips from it—watching. She steals glances, averts her eyes. She does not correct Ruchama when she makes mistakes, does not fix them either, but leaves them out in places where Ruchama will find them. It annoys Ruchama to come upon the hair she was supposed to use for the Berger wig coiled neatly on the edge of a shelf, to find the caps she sized wrong placed in the wicker basket under her desk.

Tzippy has even taken to putting things down when she means to pass them. She places the pincushion next to Ruchama instead of handing it to her. The phone rings for Ruchama, and Tzippy does it again. She carries over the cordless and puts the phone down at Ruchama's side.

"Why must you do that?" Ruchama says. She covers the mouthpiece, wants to know who's on the line.

"The messenger."

Ruchama looks at the receiver and shuts it off. "I told you never to give me that man," she says. The telephone rings again.

"Answer it," Tzippy says. "He calls ten times a day. You answer it and talk to him and then to me. I want to know why the deliveryman is so concerned about an orange tree with no oranges."

Ruchama answers the phone.

"Hello," she says. "No," she says. She walks to the back corner of the work space, the unused corner with the old storage closet where her wig is hidden. "Leave me alone," she says. "Not another cent," she says. She hangs up again, then raises her voice. "Not another penny more for that damn tree."

It is like facing her mother when she discovered Ruchama's lipstick, like sitting in the living room with both her parents after she was caught on the date Tzippy had arranged— spotted by her own father while walking down King Street and talking to a boy. Ruchama figures she is ruined and will have to tell all.

Tzippy has dragged her out to the front room and put her in a chair. She sits in the other one and talks to Ruchama around the narrow tree trunk.

"I haven't said a word, not to another soul." Tzippy is enjoying this, Ruchama thinks. She has always resented working for Ruchama and here is her chance to take control. "You doze during the day. You forget. Anything you touch has to be redone. You chased off our best client and an old friend. You chased off a woman with tons of money and a big mouth. You haven't paid the bills—don't think I didn't notice. Tell me, Ruchama, before you destroy the business that supports both our families. Open up before you destroy a friendship spanning thirty years."

Ruchama can't face her; she turns to the standing mirror and turns again to the wall of photos.

"If I must," Ruchama says, and she looks one second into the future, and then she is at the state fair bobbing for apples. And she does not, cannot, ruin the surprise. "I kissed the tree man," she says. Something so unbelievable, it's believable. Something to appeal to Tzippy's mischievous side. "He kissed me and I let him. Not once, but twice. Twice when I went to the city for supplies."

"No," Tzippy screams, hands to her mouth. She tucks her legs under her and hangs over the arm of her chair. "You didn't."

"I didn't want to, but I did."

"Shlomi!" Tzippy says. "A gentile, Ruchama. And half your age. You didn't. Your children. The man has a ring in his lip."

"Ice cold," Ruchama says. "Ice cold and red hot."

"It must stop, Ruchama."

"That is what I keep telling him."

"But he won't listen," Tzippy says. "He is so full of lust. He knows it can't be but won't listen. He wants you to meet him once more. To tell him you can't do it while looking deep into his eyes."

The admission changes everything. Tzippy works twice as hard as she ever did. Ruchama need only stay alert enough during the days to retell the lie again and again. She makes up tiny details that she adds to each version. Tzippy's hands fly as she listens, wide eyed, stopping only to gasp. She advises Ruchama against it again and again, then she plots out their future if they should decide to run away. "Would he convert, do you think? Would he look nice in a beard?" Tzippy passes things into Ruchama's hands, lingering now, offering a moment of warmth and support. She passes everything except for the phone. She hangs up on the deliveryman, who calls again and again. Sometimes she rushes out hushed advice before cutting the line. "Let it go," she says. "I know it hurts," she tells him, "but it cannot be."

Ruchama feels less guilt than she'd imagined. It's Tzippy's own fault for buying into such nonsense. And it's not without purpose. A few more weeks. One month to Passover. The wig is almost ready.

It's 8:30 in the morning when Ruchama finishes the wig. Passover is ten days away. The wig is heavier than any she's ever made, an intense and copious thing. Ruchama doesn't usually shave her head, but the vanity of such hair calls for compensation. Ruchama plugs in the electric clippers, nicks herself on the first pass.

She fits her hands into the cap and stretches it round her scalp. It holds tight. She drops her head between her knees and, using her fingertips to keep the wig in place, flips her head and feels the whole weight of the hair swinging up and over, curl after curl hitting against her back.

She forgives every flaw in the mirror. Her eyes are blood-shot and swollen, but she doesn't see it. She is amazed at how utterly striking, how truly gorgeous, is this mane of perfect hair. The weight alone, that comforting weight, the safety of the curls framing her face. It is majestic. She can't wait to sit down in front of Nava, to shake out her hair and have it pour into Nava's lap over the back of her seat. The commotion. Ruchama will get her whispering. The men will hiss for silence, and no one will talk about how she's let herself go ever again. Nava will see Ruchama's face framed like a maiden's. She will remember who is most beautiful.

Ten days is a long time. A person can die in an instant. A fire can burn up a house and a basement and a storage closet with a hidden wig. Maybe she will wear it on Shabbos. Ruchama picks up a hand mirror, turns slowly on a stool, leaning back, admiring. She will go to the city now. She will try it out.

The train is filled with late-morning commuters. Ruchama can sense them peering over their papers, can feel the men staring as they blow on their coffee, steadying briefcases between their legs.

Ruchama has Jamal's twenty-dollar bill ready, crushed in her palm. She tries to remain nonchalant, to keep the excitement from flushing her cheeks.

Before he gets to make conversation, Ruchama drops the money, grabs the magazines, and turns her back on Jamal.

"Well all right," Jamal says. "Looking fine."

"Sorry, what?" Ruchama says, turning up her nose, her first flirtation in years. She hurries to the side, unsuccessful at keeping the blush down. She can feel him leaning over the counter.

"A beauty," he says. "Come on back so I can have a real look."

Shlomi should say such a thing. Let them all call her back to see what they've been missing. She opens a magazine. She is searching for the new shampoo advertisement, somehow expecting to find herself on the page. The woman is there, playing in Central Park, hanging upside down from the monkey bars. There are many fathers in the park that day. Ruchama winks at the picture, as if they are compatriots. She and Ruchama, both cursed with gorgeous hair and the ceaseless attention it draws.

Ruchama faces up Sixth Avenue as she reads, a stray curl, then two, blown back by the wind. And then she is off, walking down King Street in her mind. All eyes are upon her, admiring. A young woman strikes her husband for turning his head. The baker comes out to the sidewalk and hands her a layer cake with a chocolate shell. The traffic on King Street slows. And then she processes it in the distance, not on King Street but on Sixth. Traffic *has* slowed. A thicket of young shrubbery has sprouted up in the middle of the street. Cars honk; a bus swerves, dodging. The bushes are on a dolly. Abandoned. She draws focus, looks closer. On Twenty-fourth, at Billy's Topless, his big bald head sticking up like a lightbulb, a bright idea moving over the crowd.

She calms herself with a breath. He only wants to see, to see up close. That is what she tells herself. He is walking over to admire her craftsmanship, and that will be that. Tzippy is right; they always must wonder what has become of their hair. They sell it to feed children. To pay gambling debts. Because they are sick of the flower shop and hold cash in their hands.

Jamal will protect her. He calls around to her right then, another flirtation.

The deliveryman gets closer and crosses his arms in the air. "Money," he calls, without picking up speed. He is half a block away, and his steady pace terrifies her, the walking so much more definite than if he were to run. "I need more money," he yells. Ruchama has worked this out a thousand times, picked this corner for just such a reason. Far enough away. If she spots a familiar face . . .

She drops the magazines into the trash basket, looks up at the walk signal, and is already moving into the flow of foot traffic. People are turning round, stepping aside to let her through.

Ruchama picks up her pace when she hits the opposite curb. She chances a quick glance. He is almost upon her.

"You stole my hair," he screams. "She stole my hair."

Ruchama puts a hand to her head and pulls off the wig. She stuffs it into her bag and clutches the bag to her chest. A mess of curls snakes out over the sides. Ruchama can feel people looking, the whole of the city watching.

Worth every penny and every shame, she thinks, for one slow spin, hair on her head and mirror in her hand, leaning back, beautiful.

The Gilgul of Park Avenue

The Jewish day begins in the calm of evening, when it won't shock the system with its arrival. It was then, three stars visible in the Manhattan sky and a new day fallen, that Charles Morton Luger understood he was the bearer of a Jewish soul.

Ping! Like that it came. Like a knife against a glass.

Charles Luger knew, as he knew anything at all, that there was a Yiddishe neshama functioning inside.

He was not one to engage taxicab drivers in conversation, but such a thing as this he felt obligated to share. A New York story of the first order, like a woman giving birth in an elevator, or a hot-dog vendor performing open-heart surgery with pocketknife and Bic pen. Was not this a rebirth in itself? It was something, he was sure. So he leaned forward in his seat, raised a fist, and knocked on the Plexiglas divider.

The driver looked into his rearview mirror.

"Jewish," Charles said. "Jewish, here in the back."

The driver reached up and slid the partition over so that it hit its groove loudly.

"Oddly, it seems that I'm Jewish. Jewish in your cab."

"No problem here. Meter ticks the same for all creeds." He pointed at the digital display.

Charles thought about it. A positive experience or, at least, benign. Yes, benign. What had he expected?

He looked out the window at Park Avenue, a Jew looking out at the world. Colors no brighter or darker, though he was, he admitted, already searching for someone with a beanie, a landsman who might look his way, wink, confirm what he already knew.

The cab slowed to a halt outside his building, and Petey the doorman was already on his way to the curb. Charles removed his money clip and peeled off a fifty. He reached over the seat, holding on to the bill.

"Jewish," Charles said, pressing the fifty into the driver's hand. "Jewish right here in your cab."

Charles hung his coat and placed his briefcase next to the stand filled with ornate canes and umbrellas that Sue—carefully scouting them out around the city—did not let him touch. Sue had redone the foyer and the living room and dining room all in chintz fabric, an overwhelming amount of flora and fauna patterns, a vast slippery-looking expanse. Charles rushed through it to the kitchen, where Sue was removing dinner from the refrigerator.

She was reading the note the maid had left, and lit burners and turned dials accordingly. Charles came up behind her. He inhaled the scent of perfume and the faint odor of cigarettes laced underneath. Sue turned and they kissed, more passionate than friendly, which was neither an everyday occurrence nor altogether rare. She was still wearing her contacts; her eyes were a radiant blue.

"You won't believe it," Charles said—surprised to find himself elated. He was a levelheaded man, not often victim to extremes of mood.

"What won't I believe?" Sue said. She separated herself from him and slipped a tray into the oven.

Sue was art director at a glossy magazine, her professional life comparatively glamorous. The daily doings of a financial analyst, Charles felt, did not even merit polite attention. He never told her anything she wouldn't believe.

"Well, what is it, Charles?" She held a glass against the recessed ice machine in the refrigerator. "Damn," she said. Charles, at breakfast, had left it set on CRUSHED.

"You wouldn't believe my taxi ride," he said, suddenly aware that a person disappointed by ice chips wouldn't take well to such a change.

"Your face," she said.

"Nothing, just remembering. A heck of a ride. A maniac. Taxi driver running lights. Up on the sidewalk. Took Third before the bridge traffic cleared."

The maid had prepared creamed chicken. When they sat down to dinner Charles stared at his plate. Half an hour Jewish and already he felt obliged. He knew there were dietary laws, milk and meat forbidden to touch, but he didn't know if chicken was considered meat and didn't dare ask Sue and chance a confrontation, not until he'd formulated a plan. He'd call Dr. Birnbaum, his psychologist, in the morning. Or maybe he'd find a rabbi. Who better to guide him in such matters?

And so, a Marrano in modern times, Charles ate his chicken like a gentile—all the while a Jew in his heart.

At work the next morning, Charles got right on it.

He pulled out the yellow pages, referenced and cross-referenced, following the "see" list throughout the phone book. More than one listing with "Zion" put him in touch with a home for the aged. "Redemption" led him farther off course. Going back to the phone book, he came upon an organization that seemed frighteningly appropriate. For one, it was a Royal Hills number, a neighborhood thick with Jews.

The listing was for the Royal Hills Mystical Jewish Reclamation Center, or, as the recorded voice said, the R-HMJRC— just like that, with a pause after the *R*. It was a sort of clearinghouse for the Judeo-supernatural: press 1 for messianic time clock, press 2 for dream interpretation and counseling, 3 for numerology, and 4 for a retreat schedule. The "and 4" took the wind out of his sails. A bad sign. Recordings never said "and 4" and then "and 5." But the message went on. A small miracle. "For all gilgulim, cases of possible reincarnation or recovered memory, please call Rabbi Zalman Meintz at the following number."

Charles took it down, elated. This is exactly why he'd moved to New York from Idaho so many years before. Exactly the reason. Because you could find anything in the Manhattan yellow pages. Anything. A book as thick as a cinder block.

The R-HMJRC was a beautifully renovated brownstone in the heart of Royal Hills. It was Gothic looking. The front steps had been widened to the width of the building, and the whole facade of the first two floors had been torn out and replaced with a stone arch, a glass wall behind it. The entry hall was marble, and Charles was impressed. There is money in the God business, he told himself, making a mental note.

Like this it went: standing in the middle of the marble floor, feeling the cold space, the only thing familiar being his unfamiliar self. And then it was back. *Ping!* Once again, understanding.

Only yesterday his whole life was his life, familiar, totally his own. Something he lived in like an old wool sweater. Today: Brooklyn, an archway, white marble.

"Over here, over here. Follow my voice. Come to the light."

Charles had taken the stairs until they ended, and entered what appeared to be an attic, slanted ceilings and dust, overflowing with attic-like stuff, chairs and a rocking horse, a croquet set and boxes, everywhere boxes—as if all the remnants of the brownstone's former life had been driven upward.

"There is a path on your right. Make your way, it's possible. I got here." The speech was punctuated with something like laughter. It was vocalized joy, a happy stutter.

The path led to the front of the building and a clearing demarcated by an Oriental screen. The rabbi sat in a leather armchair across from a battered couch—both clearly salvaged from the spoils that cluttered the room.

"Zalman," the man said, jumping up, shaking Charles's hand. "Rabbi Zalman Meintz."

"Charles Luger," Charles said, taking off his coat.

The couch, though it had seen brighter days, was clean. Charles had expected dust to rise when he sat. As soon as he touched the fabric, he got depressed. More chintz. The sun-dulled flowers crawling all over it.

"Just moved in," Zalman said. "New space. Much bigger. But haven't, as you see"—he pointed at specific things, a mirror, a china hutch—"please excuse—or forgive—please excuse our appearance. More important matters come first. Very busy lately, very busy." As if to illustrate, a phone perched on a dollhouse set to ringing. "You see," Zalman said. He reached over, turned off the ringer. "Like that all day—at night too. Busier even at night."

The surroundings didn't inspire confidence, but Zalman did. He couldn't have been much more than thirty but looked, to Charles, like a real Jew: long black beard, black suit, black hat at his side, and a nice big caricaturish nose, like Fagin's but friendlier.

"Well then, Mr. Luger. What brings you to my lair?"

Charles was still unready to talk. He turned his attention to a painted seascape on the wall. "That the Galilee?"

"Oh, no." Rabbi Meintz laughed and, sitting back, crossed his legs. For the first time Charles noticed that the man was sporting a pair of heavy wool socks and suede sandals. "That's Bolinas. My old stomping grounds."

"Bolinas?" Charles said. "California?"

"I see what's happening here. Very obvious." Zalman uncrossed his legs, reached out, and put a hand on Charles's knee. "Don't be shy," he said. "You've made it this far. Searched me out in a bright corner of a Brooklyn attic. If such a meeting has been ordained, which, by its very nature, it has been, then let's make the most of it."

"I'm Jewish," Charles said. He said it with all the force, excitement, and relief of any of life's great admissions. There was silence. Zalman was smiling, listening intently, and, apparently, waiting.

"Yes," he said, maintaining the smile, barely jarring it to speak. "And?"

"Since yesterday," Charles said. "In a cab."

"Oh," Zalman said. And, "Oh! Now I get it."

"It just came over me."

"Wild," Zalman said. He clapped his hands, looked up at the ceiling, laughed. "Miraculous."

"Unbelievable," Charles added.

"No!" Zalman said, his smile gone, a single finger held up in Charles's face. "No, it's not unbelievable. That it is not. I believe you. Knew before you said—exactly why I didn't respond. A Jew sits in front of me and tells me he's Jewish. This is no surprise. To see a man, so Jewish, a person who could be my brother, who *is* my brother, tell me he has only now discovered he's Jewish—that, my friend, that is truly miraculous." During his speech he had slowly moved his finger back, and then thrust it into Charles's face anew. "But not unbelievable. I see cases of this all the time."

"Then it's possible? That it's true?"

"Already so Jewish"—Zalman laughed—"asking questions you've already answered. You know the truth better than I do. You're the one who came to the discovery. How do you feel?"

"Fine," Charles said. "Different but fine."

"Well don't you think you'd be upset if it was wrong what

you knew? Don't you think you'd be less than fine if this were a nightmare? Somehow suffering if you'd gone crazy?"

"Who said anything about crazy?" Charles asked. Crazy, he was not.

"Did I?" Zalman said. He grabbed at his chest. "An accident, purely. Slip of the tongue. So many who come have trouble with the news at home. Their families doubt."

Charles shifted. "I haven't told her."

Zalman raised an eyebrow, turned his head to favor the accusing eye.

"There is a wife who doesn't know?"

"That's why I'm here. For guidance." Charles put his feet up on the couch, lay down like at Dr. Birnbaum's. "I need to tell her, to figure out how. I need, also, to know what to do. I ate milk and meat last night."

"First history," Zalman said. He slipped off a sandal. "Your mother's not Jewish?"

"No, no one. Ever. Not that I know."

"This is also possible," Rabbi Zalman said. "It may be only that your soul was at Sinai. Maybe an Egyptian slave that came along. But once the soul witnessed the miracles at Sinai, accepted there the word, well, it became a Jewish soul. Do you believe in the soul, Mr. Luger?"

"I'm beginning to."

"All I'm saying is that the soul doesn't live or die. It's not an organic thing like the body. It is there. And it has a history."

"And mine belonged to a Jew?"

"No, no. That's exactly the point. Jew, non-Jew, doesn't matter. The body doesn't matter. It is the soul itself that is Jewish."

They talked for over an hour. Zalman gave him books, *The Chosen*, *A Hedge of Roses*, and a copy of *The Code of Jewish Law*. Charles agreed to cancel his shrink appointment for the next day, and Zalman would come to his office to study with him. There would be payment, of course. A minor fee, expenses, some for charity and ensured good luck. The money was not the important thing, Zalman assured him. The crucial thing was having a guide to help him through his transformation. And who better than Zalman, a man who'd come to the Jewish religion the same way? Miserable in Bolinas, addicted to sorrow and drugs, he was on the brink when he discovered his Jewish soul. "And you never needed a formal conversion?" Charles asked, astounded. "No," Zalman said. "Such things are for others, for the litigious and stiff minded; such rituals are not needed for those who are called by their souls."

"Tell me then," Charles said. He spoke out of the side of his mouth, feeling confident and chummy. "Where'd you get the shtick from? You look Jewish, you talk Jewish—the authentic article. I turn Jewish and get nothing. You come from Bolinas and sound like you've never been out of Brooklyn."

"And if I'd discovered I was Italian, I'd play bocci like a pro. Such is my nature, Mr. Luger. I am most open to letting take form that which is truly inside."

This was, of course, a matter of personal experience. Zalman's own. Charles's would inevitably be different. Unique. If it was slower—the change—then let it be so. After all, Zalman counseled, the laws were not to be devoured like bonbons but to be embraced as he was ready. Hadn't it taken him fifty-five years to learn he was Jewish? Yes, everything in good time.

"Except," Zalman said, standing up. "You must tell your wife first thing. Kosher can wait. Tefillin can wait. But there is one thing the tender soul can't bear—the sacrifice of Jewish pride."

Sue had a root canal after work. She came home late, carrying a pint of ice cream. Charles had already set the table and served dinner on the off chance she might be able to eat.

"How was it?" he asked, lighting a candle, pouring the wine.

He did not tease her, did not say a word about her slurred speech or sagging face. He pretended it was a permanent injury, that it was nerve damage, acted as if it were a business dinner and Sue were a client with a crippled lip.

Sue approached the table and lifted the bottle. "Well you're not leaving me, I can tell that much. You'd never have opened your precious Haut-Brion to tell me you were running off to Greece with your secretary."

"True," he said. "I'd have saved it to drink on our veranda in Mykonos."

"Glad to see," she said, standing on her toes and planting a wet and pitifully slack kiss on his cheek, "that the fantasy has already gotten that far."

"The wine's actually a feeble attempt at topic broaching."

Sue pried the top off her ice cream and placed the carton in the center of her plate. They both sat down.

"Do tell," she said.

"I'm Jewish." That easy. It was not, after all, the first time.

"Is there a punch line?" she asked. "Or am I supposed to supply that?"

He said nothing.

"OK. Let's try it again. I'll play along. Go, give me your line."

"In the cab yesterday. I just knew. I understood, felt it for real. And—" He looked at her face, contorted, dead with anesthesia. A surreal expression to receive in return for surreal news. "And it hasn't caused me any grief. Except for my fear of telling you. Otherwise, I actually feel sort of good about it. Different. But like things, big things, are finally right."

"Let's get something out of the way first." She made a face, a horrible face. Charles thought maybe she was trying to bite her lip—or scowl. "OK?"

"Shoot."

"What you're really trying to tell me is: Honey, I'm having a nervous breakdown and this is the best way to tell you. Correct?" She plunged a teaspoon into the ice cream and came up with a massive spoonful. "If it's not a nervous breakdown, I want to know if you feel like you're clinically insane."

"I didn't expect this to go smoothly," Charles said.

"You pretend that you knew I'd react badly." Sue spoke quickly and (Charles tried not to notice) drooled. "Really though, with your tireless optimism, you thought I would smile and tell you to be Jewish. That's what you thought, Charles." She jammed her spoon back into the carton, left it buried. "Let me tell you, this time you were way off. Wrong in your heart and right in your head. It couldn't have gone smoothly. Do you know why? Do you know?"

"Why?" he asked.

"Because what you're telling me, out of the blue, out of nowhere, because what you're telling me is, inherently, crazy."

Charles nodded repeatedly, as if a bitter truth were confirmed.

"He said you would say that."

"Who said, Charles?"

"The rabbi."

"You've started with rabbis?" She pressed at her sleeping lip.

"Of course, rabbis. Who else gives advice to a Jew?"

Charles read the books at work the next day and filled a legal pad with notes. When the secretary buzzed with Dr. Birnbaum on the line inquiring about the sudden cancelation, Charles, for the first time since he'd begun his treatment fifteen thousand dollars before, did not take the doctor's call. He didn't take any, absorbed in reading *A Hedge of Roses*, the definitive guide to a healthy marriage through ritual purity, and waiting for Rabbi Zalman.

When Charles heard Zalman outside his office, he buzzed his secretary. This was a first, as well. Charles never buzzed the secretary until she had buzzed him first. There was a protocol for entry to his office. It's good for a visitor to hear buzz and counterbuzz. It sets a tone.

"So," Zalman said, seating himself. "Did you tell her?"

Charles placed his fountain pen back in its holder. He straightened the base with two hands. "She sort of half believes me. Enough to worry. Not enough to tear my head off. But she knows I'm not kidding. And she does think I'm crazy."

"And how do you feel?"

"Content." Charles leaned back in his swivel chair, his arms dangling over the sides. "Jewish and content. Excited. Still excited. The whole thing's ludicrous. I was one thing and now I'm another. But neither holds any real meaning. It's only that when I discovered I was Jewish, I think I also discovered God."

"Like Abraham," Zalman said, with a worshipful look at the ceiling. "Now it's time to smash some idols." He pulled out a serious-looking book, leather bound and gold embossed. A book full of secrets, Charles was sure. They studied until Charles told Zalman he had to get back to work. "No fifty-minute hour here," Zalman said, taking a swipe at the psychologist. They agreed to meet daily and shook hands twice before Zalman left.

He wasn't gone long enough to have reached the elevators when Walter, the CEO, barged into Charles's office, stopping immediately inside the door.

"Who's the fiddler on the roof?" Walter said.

"Broker."

"Of what?" Walter tapped his wedding band against the nameplate on the door.

"Commodities," Charles said. "Metals."

"Metals." Another tap of the ring. A knowing wink.

"Promise me something, Charley. This guy tries to sell you the steel out of the Brooklyn Bridge, at least bargain with the man."

There had been a few nights of relative quiet and a string of dinners with nonconfrontational foods. Among them: a risotto and then a blackened trout, a spaghetti squash with an eye-watering vegetable marinara, and—in response to a craving of Sue's—a red snapper with tomato and those little bits of caramelized garlic the maid did so well.

Sue had, for all intents and purposes, ignored Charles's admission and, mostly, ignored Charles. Charles spent his time in the study reading the books Zalman had brought him.

This was how the couple functioned until the day the maid left a pot of beef bourguignon.

"The meat isn't kosher and neither is the wine," Charles said, referring to the wine both in and out of his dinner. "There's a pound of bacon fat in this. I'm not complaining, only letting you know. Really. Bread will do me fine." He reached over and took a few slices from the basket, refilled his wineglass with water.

Sue glared at him.

"You're not complaining?"

"No," he said, and reached for the butter.

"Well, I'm complaining! I'm complaining right now!" Sue slammed a fist down so that her glass tipped over, spilling wine onto the tablecloth she loved. They both watched the tablecloth soak up the wine, the lace and the stitching, which fattened and swelled, the color spreading along the workmanship as if through a series of veins. Neither moved.

"Sue, your tablecloth."

"Fuck my tablecloth," she said.

"Oh my." He took a sip of water.

"Oh my is right. You bet, mister." She made a noise that Charles considered to be a growl. His wife of twenty-seven years had growled at him.

"If you think I'll ever forgive you for starting this when I was crippled with Novocain. Attacking me when I could hardly talk. If you think," she said, "if you think I'm going to start paying twelve dollars and fifty cents for a roast chicken, you are terribly, terribly wrong."

"What is this about chickens?" Charles did not raise his voice.

"The religious lady at work. She puts in orders on Wednesday. Every week she orders the same goddamn meal. A twelve-dollar-and-fifty-cent roast chicken." Sue shook her head. "You should have married an airline chef if you wanted kosher meals."

"Different fight, Sue. We're due for a fight, but I think you're veering toward the wrong one."

"Why don't you tell me then," she said. "Since all has been revealed to you, why don't you enlighten me as to the nature of the conflict."

"Honestly, I think you're threatened. So I want you to know. I still love you. You're still my wife. This should make you happy for me. I've found God."

"Exactly the problem. You didn't find our God. I'd have been good about it if you found our God—or even a less demanding one. A deity less queer." She scanned the table again, as if to find one of his transgressions left out absent-mindedly like house keys. "Today the cheese is gone. You threw out all the cheese, Charles. How could God hate cheese?"

"A woman who thinks peaches are too suggestive for the fruit bowl could give in on a quirk or two."

"You think I don't notice what's going on, that I don't notice you making ablutions in the morning?" Sue dipped her napkin into her water glass. "I've been waiting for your midlife crisis. But I expected something I could handle, a small test. An imposition. Something to rise above and prove my love for you in a grand display of resilience. Why couldn't you have turned into a vegan? Or a liberal Democrat? Slept with your secretary for real." Sue dabbed at the wine stain. "Any of those and I would've made do."

Charles scrutinized her.

"So essentially you're saying it would be OK if I changed into a West Side Jew. Like if we suddenly lived in the Apthorp."

Sue thought about it.

"Well, if you have to be Jewish, why *so* Jewish? Why not like the Browns in six-K? Their kid goes to Haverford. Why," she said, closing her eyes and pressing two fingers to her temple, "why do people who find religion always have to be so goddamn extreme?"

"Extreme," Charles felt, was too extreme a word considering all there was to know and all the laws he had yet to implement. He hadn't been to synagogue. He hadn't yet observed the Sabbath. He had only changed his diet and said a few prayers.

For this he'd been driven from his own bedroom.

Occasionally Sue sought him out, always with impeccable timing. She came into the den the first morning he donned prayer shawl and phylacteries, which even to Charles looked especially strange. The leather box and the strap twirled tightly around his arm, another box planted square in the center of his head. He was in the midst of the Eighteen Benedictions when Sue entered, and was forced to listen to her tirade in silence.

"My Charley, always topping them all," she said, watching as he rocked back and forth, his lips moving. "I've heard of wolf men and people being possessed. I've even seen modern vampires on TV. Real people who drink blood. But this beats all." She left him and then returned with a mug of coffee in hand.

"I spoke to Dr. Birnbaum. I was going to call him myself, to see how he was dealing with your change." She blew on her coffee. "Guess what, Charley. He calls me first. Apologizes for crossing boundaries, then tells me you've stopped coming, that you won't take his calls. Oh, I say, that's because Charley's Jewish and is very busy meeting with the rabbi. He's good, your shrink. Remains calm. And then, completely deadpan, he asks me—as if it makes any difference—what kind of rabbi. I told him what you told me, word for word. The kind from Bolinas. The kind who doesn't need to be ordained because he's been a rabbi in his past nine lives. And what, I asked him, does one man, one man himself ten generations a rabbi, what does he need with anyone's diploma?" Sue put the mug down on a lamp stand.

"Dr. Birnbaum's coming to dinner next week. On Monday. I even ordered kosher food, paper plates, the whole deal. You'll be able to eat in your own house like a human being. An evening free of antagonism where we can discuss this like adults. His idea. He said to order kosher food once first before leaving you. So I placed an order." She smoothed down her eyebrows, waited for a response. "You can stop your praying, Charles"—she turned to leave—"your chickens are on the way."

Charles had no suits left. Shatnez, the mixing of linen and wool, is strictly forbidden. On Zalman's recommendation, he sent his wardrobe to Royal Hills for testing and was forced to go to work the next day in slacks and suspenders, white shirt, and tie. Walter hadn't left him alone since he'd arrived. "It ain't Friday, Charley," he kept saying. "Casual day is only once a week." This he interchanged with "Why go to so much trouble? A nicely pressed bathrobe would be fine."

Charles had worked himself into a funk by the time Zalman entered his office. He'd accomplished nothing all morning.

"I am weakening," Charles said. "The revelation lasts about a second, comes and goes, a hot flash in the back of a taxi. But the headache it leaves you with—a whopper of a headache—that persists."

Zalman scratched at his nostril with a pinkie, a sort of refined form of picking. "Were you in a fraternity in college?"

"Of course," Charles said.

"Then consider this pledging. You've been tapped, given a bid, and now is the hard part before all the good stuff. Now's when you buy the letters on the sly and try them on at home in front of the mirror."

"Wonderful, Zalman. Well put. But not so simple. I've got to tell my boss something soon. And tensions have risen at home. We're having dinner on Monday. My wife and my shrink versus me. She's even ordered kosher food, trying to be friendly about it."

"Kosher food." A knee-slapper, a big laugh. "The first step. Doesn't sound anything but positive to me. By any chance, has she gone to the ritual bath yet?"

Charles spun his chair around, looked out the window, then, slowly, spun it back.

"Zalman," he said, "that's a tough one. And it sort of makes me think you're not following. Sue refuses to go for a couple of reasons. One because she hates me, and our marriage is falling apart. And two, she maintains—and it's a valid point, a fairly good argument—that she's not Jewish."

"I see."

"I want you to come on Monday, Zalman. A voice of reason will come in handy after the weekend. I'm going to keep my first Shabbos. And if Sue remains true to form, I'm in for a doozy."

"Find out where the food is from. If it's really kosher catered, I'll be there."

The clocks had not changed for the season, and Shabbos still came early. Charles put on his suit jacket—deemed kosher— and his coat and went home without explanation. He didn't touch the candlesticks on the mantelpiece, didn't risk raising Sue's ire. Instead he dug a pair, dented and tarnished, from a low cabinet in the overstuffed and unused butler's pantry. The maid passed, said nothing. She took her pocketbook and the day's garbage into the service hall.

In the absence of wife or daughter, the honor of ushering in the Sabbath falls upon the lone man. Charles cleared a space on the windowsill in the study and, covering his eyes before the lit candles, made the blessing. He paused at the place where the woman is permitted to petition the Lord with wishes and private blessings, and stood, palms cool against his eyes, picturing Sue.

The candles flickered next to the window, burning lopsided and fast.

Charles extended the footrest on his recliner. He closed his eyes and thought back to his first night away from home, sleeping on a mattress next to his cousin's bed. He was four or five, and his cousin, older, slept with the bedroom door shut tight, not even a crack of light from the hallway. It was the closest to this experience, the closest he could remember to losing and gaining a world.

The candles were out when Charles heard Sue pass on her way to the bedroom. He tried to come up with a topic of conversation, friendly and day to day. He came up with nothing, couldn't remember what they'd talked about over their life together. What had they said to each other when there was nothing pressing? What had they chatted about for twenty-seven years?

He got up and went to her.

Sue was sitting at the far window on the petite antique chair that was intended only to be admired. She held a cigarette and flicked the ash into a small porcelain dish resting on her knee. In half silhouette against the electric dusk of the city, Sue appeared as relaxed as Charles had seen her since long before his revelation. He could tell, or thought he could, that she was concentrating on ignoring his presence. She would not have her moment of peace compromised.

This was his wife. A woman who, if she preferred, could pretend he was not there. A woman always able to live two realities at once. She could spend a day at work slamming down phones, storming down hallways with layouts she'd torn in half, then come home to entertain, serve dinner, pass teacups in a way that hushed a room.

How was he to explain his own lack of versatility? Here was a woman who lived in two generations simultaneously. How was he to make clear his struggle living in one? And how to tell the woman of two lives that he had invited over Zalman, who carried in his soul a full ten?

On Sunday Charles was reading a copy of Leon Uris's *QB VII* when Sue ran—truly ran—into the study and grabbed him by the arm. He was shocked and made the awkward movements of someone who is both dumbfounded and manhandled at the very same time, like a tourist mistakenly seized by the police.

"Sue, what are you doing?"

"I could kill you," she said. And though smaller, she had already pulled him to his feet. Charles followed her to the foyer.

"What is this?" she yelled, slamming open the door.

"A mezuzah," he said. "If you mean that." He pointed at the small metal casing nailed to the doorpost. "I need it," he said. "I have to kiss it."

"Oh my God," she said, slamming the door closed, giving the neighbors no more than a taste. "My God!" She steadied herself, put a hand against the wall. "Well where did it come from? It's got blue paint on it. Where does one buy a used mezuzah?"

"I don't know where to get one. I pried it off eleven-D with a letter opener. They don't even use it. Steve Fraiman had me in to see their Christmas tree last year. Their daughter is dating a black man."

"Are you insane? Five years on the waiting list to get into this building and now you're vandalizing the halls. You think anyone but me will believe your cockamamy story? Oh, I'm not a Nazi, Mrs. Fraiman, just a middle-aged man who woke up a Jew."

"It happened in a cab. I didn't wake up anything."

Sue put her other hand against the wall and let her head hang.

"I've invited the rabbi," Charles said.

"You think that's going to upset me? You think I didn't know you'd drag him into this? Good, bring him. Maybe they have a double open at Bellevue."

"This is very intolerant, Sue." He reached out to touch her.

"Go back to the study," she said. "Go paw one of your books."

They considered the table. Charles and Sue stood at opposite ends, appraising the job the maid had done.

It was admirable.

There was a paper tablecloth and paper cups and plastic champagne glasses with snap-on bases. There were patterned paper napkins that matched the pattern on the plates, plastic forks and plastic spoons, and a few other things—cheap but not disposable. Knives, for instance, the knives were real, new, wooden-handled steak knives. Sue had even gone to the trouble of finding a decent bottle of kosher wine. One bottle. The other was a blackberry. Charles wondered if the blackberry was a warning as to what continued religiosity might do to the refined palate. Screw-top wine. Sugary plonk. He was going to comment, but looking again at the lavish spread, both leaves inserted into the table, the polished silver on the credenza, he reconsidered. It was more than a truce. It was an attempt to be open—or at least a request that the maid make it resemble as much.

"Mortifying," she said. "Like a child's birthday party. We've got everything except for a paper donkey tacked to the wall."

"I appreciate it, Sue. I really, really do." He had sweetness in his voice, real love for the first time since he'd made his announcement.

"Eighty-eight dollars' worth of the blandest food you've ever had. The soup is inedible, pure salt. I had a spoonful and needed to take an extra high-blood-pressure pill. I'll probably die before dinner's over, and then we'll have no problems."

"More and more," Charles said, taking a yarmulke from his pocket and fastening it to his head, "more and more, you're the one that sounds like a Jew."

When Charles answered the knock on the study door, he was surprised to find Zalman standing there, surprised that Sue hadn't come to get him.

"She is very nice, your wife," Zalman said. "A sensible woman, it appears."

"Appearances are important," Charles said.

Zalman brightened, and exuded joy as he did.

"It will be fine," he said. He hooked Charles's arm into his own and led him down the hall.

Sue and Dr. Birnbaum—sporting a yellow sweater—were already seated. Charles sat at the head of the table, and Zalman stood behind his chair.

The most painful silence Charles had ever experienced ensued. He was aware of his breathing, his pulse and temperature. He could feel the contents of his intestines, the blood in his head, the air settling on his eardrums, lake-smooth without sound.

It was Zalman who spoke.

"Is there a place where I can wash?" he asked.

Before eating bread, Charles knew.

"Yes," Charles said. "I'll come too."

He looked at Sue as he got up. Charles knew what she was thinking.

Say it, he wanted to tell her. Point it out to Dr. Birnbaum. You're right. It's true.

Ablutions.

Ablutions all the time.

Rabbi Zalman made a blessing over the bread, and Dr. Birnbaum muttered, "Amen."

Sue just stared. A man with a beard, a long black beard and sidelocks, was sitting in her house. Charles wanted to tell her she was staring but stopped himself with "Sue."

"What!" she said. "What, Charles?"

"Shall we eat?"

"Yes," Zalman said, his smile broad, his teeth bright white and Californian. "Let's eat first. We can discuss better on full stomachs." Reaching first one way and then the other, Zalman picked up a bottle and poured himself a brimming glass of blackberry wine.

They ate in a lesser but still oppressive silence. All showed it in their countenances, except for Zalman, who was deeply involved in the process of eating and paused only once, to say "Jewish name—Birnbaum," before going back to his food. The other three took turns looking from one to the other and back to their plates. There was a lot of staring at Zalman when there was nowhere to put their eyes.

"The barley is delicious." Dr. Birnbaum smiled as if Sue had cooked any of the food.

"Thank you," she said, snatching the empty container from next to Zalman and heading to the kitchen for another. Dr. Birnbaum took that opportunity to broach the topic with Charles.

"I don't think it's unfair to say I was startled by your news."

"Just your everyday revelation, nothing special."

"Even so, I would have hoped you'd feel comfortable discussing it with me. After all this time."

Sue returned with a quart container of barley, the plastic top in her hand. Charles cleared his throat and then there was quiet. She cocked her head. A slight tilt, an inquisitive look. Had there ever been silence at one of her dinner parties? Had her presence ever brought a conversation to an abrupt end?

She slammed the container onto the table, startling Zalman (he looked up at her and removed a bit of barley from his beard).

"I was about to explain my presence," Dr. Birnbaum said. "Let Charles know that there's no secret agenda. This isn't a competency hearing. And I'm not packing a syringe full of Thorazine."

"That was before," Sue said. "Last week, before your patient started pilfering Judaica. Before he started mortifying me in this building. Do you know that on Friday night he rode the elevator up and down like an idiot waiting for someone to press our floor? Like a retarded child. He gets in the elevator and keeps explaining it to everyone, 'Can't press the button on my Sabbath, ha ha.' He can't ask people outright, because you're only allowed to *hint*."

"Very good," Zalman said. "A fine student."

"You," she said to Zalman. "Interloper!" And then, turning back to Dr. Birnbaum, "I heard it from old Mrs. Dallal. She's the one who pressed the button. Our poor old next-door neighbor forced to ride the elevator with this maniac. She told me she was talking to Petey the doorman and couldn't figure out why the elevator door kept opening and Charley wouldn't come out. She told me that she actually asked him, 'Do you want to come out?' Now is that insane, Doctor, or is it not? Do sane people need to be invited out of elevators, or do they just get out on their own?"

Charles spoke first:

"She turned the light off in the bathroom on Friday night. She knows I can't touch the lights. I had to go in the dark. It's malicious."

"We are at the table, Charles. Paper plates or not. A man who holds his fork like an animal or not, we shall have some manners."

Zalman laughed out loud at Sue's insult.

"Those are manners, embarrassing a guest?" Now Charles yelled. "And a rabbi, yet."

"He, Charley, is not even Jewish. And neither are you. One need not be polite to the insane. As long as you don't hose them down, all is in good taste."

"She's malicious, Doctor. She brought you here to watch her insult me."

"If I'm supposed to put my two cents in," Dr. Birnbaum said, "I suppose now is the time."

"Two cents?" Zalman said. "What does that come out to for you, a consonant?"

"Thank you," the doctor said. "A perfect example of the inane kind of aggression that can turn a conversation into a brawl."

"It's because you're not wearing a tie," Charles said. "How can you control people without a tie?"

"I'm not trying to control anyone."

"It's true," Zalman said. "I went to a shrink for twelve years. Started in seventh grade. They don't control. They absolve. Like atheist priests. No responsibility for your actions, no one to answer to. Anarchists with advanced degrees." Zalman spoke right to the doctor. "You can't give people permission to ignore God. It is not your right."

"Sir," Dr. Birnbaum said. "Rabbi. As Charles's spiritual adviser, I invite you to join me in trying to help the situation."

"Exactly why I'm here," Zalman said. He pushed his chair back, rested his elbows on the table. "There is one way to help and that is to give Charles your blessing or whatever you call it. Shrinks always say it's OK, so tell him it's OK, tell her it's OK, and then all will be better."

"I can't do that—don't, in fact, do that," the doctor said. He addressed his patient. "Should we go into another room and talk?"

"If I wanted that, I'd have come to our sessions. All the therapy in the world could not bring the simple comfort that I've found in worshiping God."

"Listen to this," Sue said. "Do you hear the kind of thing I have to endure? Palaver!" The doctor looked at Sue, raised his hand, and patted the air.

"I'm listening," he said. "I actually *do* want to hear it. But from him. That Charles has gone from Christian nonbeliever to Orthodox Jew is clear. It is also perplexing." He spoke in sensible rhythms. The others listened, all primed to interrupt. "I came to dinner to hear from Charles why he changed."

"Because of his soul," Zalman said, throwing his arms up in

frustration. "He's always had this soul. His way of thinking has always been agreeable, it is only that now God let him know He wasn't pleased with the way Charley was acting."

"It's true," Charles said. "That's how it feels, like it was always in me, but that now it's time for me to do God-pleasing work."

Sue didn't speak but clenched her whole body, fists and shoulders and teeth.

"And God-pleasing work is living the life of the Orthodox Jew?" The doctor was all softness. "Are you sure it might not be something else—like gardening or meditation? Have you considered philanthropy, Charley, I mean, as a for-instance?"

"Do you not see what he is doing?" Zalman said. "The sharp tongue of the philosopher." Zalman jumped to his feet. The table shook under his weight, though silently, devoid of the usual collection of silver and crystal and robbing him of some drama. "Tell him what the King of the Khazars told his own sharp-tongued philosopher five hundred years ago." He pointed an accusing finger. "Thy words are convincing, yet they do not correspond to what I wish to find."

"Just shut up. Would you, please?" Sue said.

"It's all right, Zalman," Charles said. And Zalman sat. "It's not how I would have put it," Charles said, "but it's how I feel. You see, Doctor—with your eyes, I mean. You see how I look, how I'm acting. No different than before. Different rituals, maybe. Different foods. But the same man. Only that I feel peaceful, fulfilled."

As Charles spoke, Sue slipped from her chair, slid to the floor as might a drunk. She did not fall over, but rested on her knees, interlocking fingers and bowing her head.

She rested in the traditional Christian pose of prayer. His wife who was mortified by a white purse after Labor Day was on her knees in front of company.

"Sue, what are you doing? Get up off the floor."

She raised her chin but kept her eyes shut.

"What?" she said. "Do you have a monopoly on God? Are you the only one who can pray?"

"Point taken. Your point is taken."

"There is no point," she said. "I understand now. You were as desperate as I've become. God is for the desperate. For when there is nothing left to do."

"There is always something," Zalman said. No one acknowledged him.

"There are options, Sue." Charles was perspiring through his shirt.

Sue opened her eyes and sat on the floor, leaning on an arm, her legs at her side.

"No," she said. She did not cry, but all could tell that if she hit the wrong note, the wrong word, if she was in any way agitated further, she would lose her composure completely. "You don't seem to understand, Charles. Because you don't want to. But I do not have any idea what to do."

If there was one sacrifice Charles thought she would not be able to make it was this, to be open in front of outsiders, to look tired and overworked in front of a table set with paper plates.

"Is that what you want to hear, Charles? I'm not resigned to a goddamn thing. I'm not going to kill you or have you committed or dragged up to the summer house for deprogramming." Charles was at once relieved and frightened—for she had clearly considered her options. "But I will, Charley, be thinking and waiting. You can't stop me from that. I'm going to hope and pray. I'll even pray to your God, beg Him to make you forget Him. To cast you out."

"That's wrong, Sue." It sounded wrong.

"No, Charles. It's fair. More fair than you've been to me. You have an epiphany and want everyone else to have the same one. Well, if we did, even if it was the best, greatest, holiest thing in the world. If every person had the same one, the most you would be left with is a bright idea."

"I don't know if that's theologically sound," Zalman said, twisting the pointed ends of his beard.

"It's wonderful," the doctor said. He had a look on his face full of pride.

Charles got down on the floor and sat cross-legged in front of Sue. "What does that mean, Sue? What does it mean for me?"

"It means that your moment of grace has passed. Real or not. It's gone now. You are left with life—daily life. I'm only letting you know that as much as you worry about staying in God's favor, you should worry about staying in mine. It's like taking a new lover, Charles. You're as dizzy as a schoolgirl. But remember which one of us dropped into your life and which of us has been in for the long haul. I *am* going to try and stick it out. But let me warn you. As quick as God came into your life, I might one day be gone."

"I can't live that way," Charles said.

"That is what I go to sleep wishing."

Out of the corner of his eye Charles caught Dr. Birnbaum trying to slip out of the room without interrupting the conversation's flow. He watched the doctor recede, backing away with quiet steps, then turned to Sue. He turned to her and let all the resentment he felt come into his face. He let the muscles go, felt his eyelids drop and harden, spoke to her as intimately as if Zalman were not there.

"The biggest thing that ever happened to me, and you make me feel as if I should have kept it to myself."

She considered it. "True. It would have been better. I would much rather have found a box after you were gone: prayer books and skullcaps, used needles and women's underwear. At this point, at my age, it would have been easier to find it all after you were gone."

Charles looked to Zalman, who was, like the doctor, slowly making an exit.

"You're leaving me too?"

"Not as elegant as the doctor, but not so stupid as to miss when it's time to go."

"One minute," Charles said to his wife. "One minute and I'll be back," he pleaded, untucking his legs. "I'll walk him to the door. Our guest."

Charles followed the rabbi down the front hallway. Zalman put on his coat and tilted his hat forward, an extra edge against the city below.

"This is a crucial time," Charles said.

They were by the umbrella stand. Zalman pulled out a cane. He scratched at his nose with a pinkie. "It's an age-old problem. To all the great ones, tests are given. I wouldn't be surprised if the King of the Khazars faced the same one."

"What happened to the king?" Charles asked. "How does it turn out for the great ones?"

Zalman leaned the cane against the wall.

"It doesn't matter. The point is they all had God. They knew in their hearts God."

Charles put a hand on Zalman's shoulder. "I'm only asking for you to tell me."

"You already know," he said. The joy drained from his face. "You know but want me to lie."

"Is that so bad?"

The rabbi's face looked long and soft; the rapture did not return. "No hope, Mr. Luger. I tell you this from one Jew to another. There is no hope for the pious."

Charles made his way back to the table only to find Sue gone, the table clean, and the chairs in place. Could it have been more than a minute? He saw the garbage can from the pantry in the middle of the kitchen, the paper tablecloth sticking out the top. A disposable dinner, the dining room as if untouched.

He started toward the bedroom and stopped at the study door. Sue was standing by the windowsill beside the tarnished candlesticks which were fused in place where the wax had run off the bases. She picked at the hardened formations, forcing her nail underneath and lifting them away from the painted wood of the sill.

"It's not sacrilegious, I hope?" She continued picking at the wax that ran over the silver necks in braids.

"No," Charles said. "I don't believe it is."

He crossed the room to stand beside Sue. He reached over for the hand that scratched at the fine layers of wax on the sill. "So it'll stay there," he said. "So what."

"It will ruin the paint," she said.

"It will make the window frame look real. Like someone lives in the apartment and uses this room."

Charles looked around the study, at the lamp and the bookcase, then out the window at the buildings and the sky. He had not read that far into the Bible and still thought God might orchestrate his rescue.

He took hold of Sue's other hand and held them both in place. He wanted her to understand that there had indeed been a change of magnitude, but that the mark it left was not great. The real difference was contained in his soul, after all.

Sue's gaze fell past him before meeting his eyes.

He tried to appear open before her, to allow Sue to observe him with the profound clarity he had only so recently come to know. Charles was desperate with willingness. He struggled to stand without judgment, to be only for Sue, to be wholly seen, wanting her to love him changed.

Reb Kringle

Buna Michla stuck her head into the men's section of the sanctuary, hesitant, even though her husband was the only man there.

"Itzi," she said.

He was over by the ark, changing the bulb in the eternal light, pretending that he hadn't heard.

"Itzi, the children. Think of all the children."

"Bah!" He screwed in the bulb with his handkerchief and the eternal light flickered once before resuming its usual glow. Reb Yitzhak folded his hankie carefully and, slipping a hand under his caftan, stuffed it into his back pocket.

"Itzi!"

He turned to face her. "I should worry over the children? These are my children, all of them, that I should worry over them and their greed?"

She walked to the heart of the sanctuary and sat in the front row of the easterly-facing benches. "You should worry maybe over your shul. You should worry over the mortgage that is due." Buna took a deep breath. It was satisfying to yell at this stubborn man.

"How many people pray here, Yitzeleh? How many prayers go up to heaven from under this roof?"

"There are thirty-one people who pray here three times a day, and I don't know how many prayers reach heaven. If I knew such things I would also know a better way to pay the rent."

"And what of the roof under which we sleep?"

"Yes, Buna. And I would know also how to pay for the roof."

"How to pay you already know," she said. "Four weeks' work is food in our mouths, so what's the question? For eleven months you won't be forced to smile."

Reb Yitzhak considered his wife's statement. Every year it was the same argument and every year he lost. If only he had been born a wiser man—or married a simpler woman. He put his fingers into his long white beard and slowly worked them down toward its jagged end.

"It's a sin, this job," was all he came up with.

"It is absolutely not a sin. Where does it say that playing with goyishe children is a sin? There is no rule against playing games with them."

"Playing! You haven't seen, Buna. Anyone who has seen would never call such mayhem playing. Not since the time of Noah has the world seen such boundless greed."

"So it's not playing. Fine. But you're going. And you will be jolly and laugh like the bride's father at a wedding—miserable or not."

Reb Yitzhak took off his caftan and made his way down to the basement, leaning against the banister with every step. He was a heavy man, big in the belly, and his sciatica was acting up. The rickety wood stairs groaned as he headed down into the darkness, where he grabbed at the air in search of the frayed string and the lone sixty-watt bulb.

The oil burner sat under a web of rusted pipes that spread across the low ceiling. Behind the burner, there was a turn in the basement leading to a narrow dead end of storage space. It was the farthest place from anything, the best place to keep the Passover dishes so that they shouldn't be contaminated during the rest of the year.

He pulled the sheets off the boxes, all of which were marked PESACH, in Hebrew, with a big black marker. He couldn't make out the word since the light from the bulb barely reached that part of the room. But Reb Yitzhak didn't need to see so well. What he was looking for was recognizable by feel. The box he needed was fancy, not like the kind one brings home from the alley behind the supermarket, the sides advertising cereals and toilet paper, boxes living already a second life. This one had a top to it, the kind that could be lifted off, like a hatbox but square. This box felt smooth to the touch, overlaid with satin. When his fingers brushed against it he knew.

As he picked up the box, Reb Itzik employed the Back-Saver Erect Spine Lift, counting out the positions, "One, feet apart; two, bend knees," exactly as Dr. Mittleman had shown him.

Trudging up the stairs and directly to the front door, Itzik stopped and put the cumbersome package down.

"Ach," he said, "subway tokens."

"They're on the shelf in the foyer where they sit every day for the last forty years." Buna came in from the kitchen, wringing her hands on a towel and ready to show this mule of a man where was a token and the shelf and also, if need be, the front door.

"To get to the subway you remember?" she asked, daring him to show even the slightest bit of resistance. "You want I should get dressed and ride all the way into the city with you?"

Reb Yitzhak didn't want that at all.

Putting on caftan and coat and lifting the satin box, he gave Buna Michla his best look of despair—a look she saw only twice a year. First when it came time to carry up all the Passover dishes from the basement and, second, from the doorway, when he went off to the department store at the start of the holiday rush. So sad was the look that she lost her resolve not to chide him—she could not stand when he indulged himself to such a degree.

"Do they make you work on Shabbos?" she said. "Do they force you to go around with your head uncovered or deny you proper respect?" She undid the lock for him. "Like a king on a throne they treat you."

Itzik lifted up his box and fumbled with the door. "I pity such a king."

Leaning against a public telephone on the sidewalk and taking a moment to catch his breath, Itzik was surprised to see a new man yank open the gate of the service elevator at the department store. Ramirez, who had been there every year from the start, from the day Reb Itzik had surfaced with the employment agency slip in his hand, was now gone. He had been Reb Itzik's one friend at the job and had always kept an eye out on "the rabbi's" behalf. Without Ramirez there chewing on a cigar and offering immediate consolation, Itzik gave in to a moment of virtual despair. He felt abandoned. But at least one of them was free of the place.

Itzik approached the freight elevator, scowling at the Salvation Army worker who shook out Christmas tunes with wooden-handled bells—his last chance to be grumpy that day. The elevator man, not much older than a boy, gave Itzik a slow looking over, working his way up from the orthopedic shoes and taking his time with the long white beard. Itzik didn't flinch. He was used to it, prepared for the thousands of looks and inane questions, tugs and sticky fingers, that he was in for during the coming days.

"Floor?" the man asked, motioning with his thumb.

"Eight," Reb Itzik said.

"I heard about you," the elevator man told him, shoving the empty garbage dollies to the back wall. "You that Rabbi Santa."

"Yes," Itzik answered. "I'm the infamous Reb Santa."

The elevator man began to cough into his fist.

"Damn," he said. "I thought they were shitting me. That you was a myth."

"I exist, yes, for real," Reb Itzik said.

"Seems so," the man said. He began to pull the gate closed behind Reb Itzik and hesitated midway. "Don't you want to go in through the chimney?"

Reb Itzik turned to face the street.

"Such jokes my friend Ramirez got tired of making when you were still too small to reach the buttons."

The elves were in place, stationed every few feet throughout the giant room and continuing along the line of children that reached out into the hallway and past the tiny café, then snaked around the back of the passenger elevators and onto the staircase to the seventh floor. The room itself was decked with flashing lights and fake trees, hollow gifts with colored bows and giant paper candy canes that all the curious children ventured to lick, one germy tongue after another. There were elves posted on each side of Itzik; one—a humorless, muscular midget—wore a pair of combat boots that gave him the look of elf-at-arms. His companion might have been a twin. He wore black high-tops but had the same vigilant paramilitary demeanor.

Sitting in the chair, resting his hands on the golden armrests and leaning back against the plush cushions, Itzik was forced to admit that Buna was right. Poised in front of hundreds of worshiping faces and with a staff of thirty at his beck and call, it did indeed seem, looking down from his giant gilt chair, that he was a king on a throne.

Itzik had arranged for his support elves to keep up a steady stream of Merry Christmases. He was not one of the provincial Jews who had never crossed the Royal Hills bridge into Manhattan, the naives who'd never dealt with the secular world; it was not the first time that he'd put on the suit, and he very well knew the holiday kept him afloat. But even after all those years, the words "Merry Christmas" remained obscene to him.

The first child was an excited little girl. Small enough that she was there to see Santa, to get a pinch on the cheeks and a picture to put up on the refrigerator door—not yet a rapacious little beast with a list of demands who would have a seizure if he did not promise everything he was asked.

Itzik fell into character and gave a nod to the elf manning the crimson cord. The little girl rushed toward him like a bull in a chute, her mother prodding her regardless, and the immense crowd taking a baby step toward him, beginning with the front and then spreading backward in a seemingly endless wave.

"Ho, ho, ho," Itzik said, offering a hand as the girl was lowered into his lap. The girl beamed appropriately, bathed in the light of popping flashes and the glory of receiving the first ho, ho, ho of the year.

"What's your name?"

"It's Emily, Santa. I wrote you a letter."

"Yes, of course. The letter from Emily." He tapped his foot against the platform. "Well, remind Santa again: Have you been a good little girl?"

By twenty minutes to lunch, Itzik was sure that his very spirit was being challenged, as if God had become sadistic in his tests of the human soul. Both his pant legs were wet with the accidents of children who showed their excitement like puppies. The sciatica was broken glass running up and down the nerve in the back of his thigh. And one boy—a little Nazi, that one—had pulled out a pair of safety scissors and gone after his beard.

"Get on up there," said the elf on winter break from Tulane. She lowered a curly-headed tyke onto Itzik's left knee, his bottom lip flapping as he primed his crying machine.

"Don't cry, boychik. Tell me where's your mother."

"She's waiting for me at the Lancôme counter." And then, after a pause, "She's getting her face done."

"Her face done?" Itzik said.

"Yes," the boy said.

"So, nu?" Itzik said. "Have you been good this year?"

The boy nodded.

"Did you pay federal and state taxes, both?"

The boy shook his head, no.

"I can find it in my heart to forgive you," Itzik said. "But Santa isn't the IRS."

The boy didn't laugh. The elves didn't laugh. Tulane actually sneered.

Reb Itzik ran his hand along the length of his beard and extended his free leg.

"What can I do you for?" he asked.

"Mountain bike," said the boy.

"And?"

"Force Five Action Figures."

"And?"

"Doom—the Return of the Deathbot; Man Eater; Stop That Plague; and Gary Barry's All Star Eye on the Prize—all on CD-ROM."

"Anything else?" This appeared to be, aside from the sappy children in search of world peace, the shortest appointment of the day.

"Come on," Itzik said, "out with it." The lip was starting to move again and Itzik knew if he didn't get that last wish soon, he was in for a tantrum. "How about it?"

"A menorah," said the boy, and the tears started anyway and then stopped in a fine show of strength. It was Santa, at first stunned, then desperately trying to recall a toy by that name, who found himself bordering on a fit.

"A what?" he said, way too loudly. Then, sweet, nice, playing the part of Mr. Kringle, "A what-did-you-say?"

"A menorah."

"And what would a nice Christian boy want with a menorah?"

"I'm Jewish, not Christian. My new father says we're having a real Christmas and a tree, and not any candles at all—which isn't fair because my last father let me have a menorah and he wasn't Jewish." And the tears started running along with his nose.

"Why won't this new daddy let you light candles?"

"Because he says there's not going to be Chanukah this year."

Itzik gasped, and the boy, responding, began to bawl.

"Calm down there, little one. Santa's right here." Reaching back and squirming in his chair, Itzik produced a clean hankie. "Blow," he said, holding it to the child's nose. The child blew with some force. "Now don't you worry about a thing. You ask Santa for Chanukah, you get it." He tried his best to sound cheery, but he could feel the fury rattling in the back of his voice. "You just tell me your address and I'll bring you the candles myself."

The boy had quieted down some, but did not answer.

"Upper West or East?" Santa asked.

The boy emitted a high-pitched "Neither."

"Not in the Village, I hope," Santa said.

"We'll be in Vermont for Christmas. We have to drive all the way there so we can go to his stupid parents' church." Right then, Itzik knew, in an already fading flash of total clarity, that the farce had finally come to an end.

"Church," he said, his voice booming. "Church and no Chanukah!" Itzik yelled, scooping the boy off his knee and getting to his feet. Itzik, glaring, held the child under his arm. The elf with the high-tops took the boy and stood him up on the platform as Itzik again yelled, "No Chanukah!"

This Buna would understand; hearing this she would understand why the whole thing, the job and the costume and the laughter, was a sin. It was blasphemy! And then he screamed, loud and long, because of the cramps in his legs and the sciatic nerve that felt as if it had been stretched and released like the hemp cord of an archer's bow.

"Where is this mother?" he called out over the crowd. Grabbing the boy and risking a pinch to the already inflamed nerve, Itzik lifted him by the arm off the ground. "Where is this father?" Itzik demanded, the boy dangling like a purse in his hand. He wanted this grinch of a man brought forth, presented to him in judgment.

The boy wriggled his way free. He took a cellular phone from his pocket and called his mother on the first floor.

Itzik, conscious of the phone, began to feel guilty for scaring the child. He was still furious but also ashamed. He lowered his eyes and found the throng of holiday shoppers and the startled tots, eyes wide, staring back. Itzik, seeking a friendly face, a calm face, found none. He knew he had crossed the boundaries of propriety, and he was far past the point where he could sit back down and nod toward the elf in the combat boots to set loose the next child in line. He grabbed the pom-pom hanging down from his head and yanked off his hat, revealing a large black yarmulke.

"This," he yelled from deep down in his ample belly, "is not a fit job for a Jew."

A woman toward the middle of the room fainted dead away without letting go of the hand of her wailing daughter. She fell atop a padded rope that pulled down the brass-plated poles, spreading panic through the already jittery crowd, which began to knock over the aluminum trees and towering candy canes. The elves scurried, cursing and shrieking, unprepared by their half-day course for such an emergency. And one elf, the undercover security elf, clasped the earplug in his pointy ear and began to whisper furiously into his green velvet collar, an action that brought on the entrance of two more elves, one big and black, the other smaller, stockier, and white as the fake snow.

The pair tackled the Jewish Santa, the impostor, only kept on by the store out of fear. It had been a bad idea from the beginning, authentic beard or not; a very terrible idea from the very first year. And they would have been rid of him, too, would have been rid of Itzik ten times over, if not for the head-lock that management was in. The department store had only in September paid out two-point-three million dollars for giving the boot to HIV Santa, and it didn't have a penny more for Reb Santa or Punjabi Santa—didn't yet have an inkling about how to handle the third application from Ms. Santa that had, this time, been submitted by her counsel.

As Itzik was hustled away, his replacement, tuna-fish sandwich still in hand, was pushed in through a side door. The boy's mother fought her way in from the back of what had been the line. Wielding her shopping bags like battle-axes, she moved toward her son. She called his name with the force of a terrified parent, so loudly that it carried over the echoing hysteria of the crowd, so that Itzik heard it and knew to whom the voice belonged. Reaching the boy, she stroked his hair, and finding the throne empty and her son seemingly unharmed, she asked the question to which every mother fears the answer.

"Matthew dear, tell me the truth. Did Santa Claus touch you?"

They held him in a storeroom, in a chair neither gilt nor comfortable. The chair was in a clearing surrounded by towering walls of boxes that looked more precarious than the walls of

Jericho on Joshua's sixth pass. Itzik sat with his suit undone, the patent-leather belt hanging at his sides along with his ritual fringes. The pale security guard, a bitter elf, chided him for his lack of professionalism in the face of duty, telling Itzik he was lower than the Muscatel Santas on the street—a travesty in red.

"Better than to hang up my beard on a hook every night," Itzik said. He waited with the elf for the chief Santa to arrive.

Chief Santa was as much of a shock to Reb Itzik as Reb Itzik was to all the children, for the wizard behind this Christmas empire was not fat or jolly or even a man, but a small thin-lipped woman, without the slightest paunch from which to laugh, whose feet had clearly never donned a curly-toed bootee.

She handed him an envelope.

"Check," she said, with such great force that Itzik half expected to see a waiter rush through the door.

"You," she said, the thin lips so white with tension that her face seemed an uninterrupted plane below the nose. "You are a disgrace to the profession! And as far as we, and all of our one-hundred-and-six satellite stores are concerned, you are no longer Santa Claus."

It's not as simple as that, he wanted to tell her. Granting wishes that you don't have to make good on is simple. Believing every child who says he wasn't naughty but nice also can be done with little effort. But telling the man in the red suit—the only one in your employ with a real belly, the only one whose beard does not drip glue—that he is not Santa Claus is another matter completely. That, this woman hadn't the power to decide; Reb Yitzhak from Royal Hills, Brooklyn, hadn't the power to decide. The only one who could make such a decision was Buna Michla herself, and she had said that Itzik would finish out the year. This was the truth, he knew, as well as he knew that, sciatica or not, he would be carrying Passover dishes up from the basement again in the spring.

Itzik considered what would be worse as he rode down the

freight elevator. He leaned the satin box against an empty garment rack, the naked hangers banging against each other like bones. He pictured himself riding the subway the next morning with the apology Buna Michla had coached him on, or rejected and cleaning the pews in his costume with Buna standing over him. She'd see to it. Itzik was Santa until the end of the season, whether he lost his throne or not.

The Last One Way

I

Electrolysis promises permanence, hair killed at the roots. As far as Gitta could tell, in eighteen years of weekly visits not a single hair had been dissuaded from growing. Still she crossed to the Italian edge of Royal Hills each week and lay back on the cracked Naugahyde table in Lili's makeshift salon. They talked. Lili shocked and plucked. Then Gitta made her way home red faced and tender, the crisp sting of witch hazel humming in electrified pores.

Gitta never blamed Lili, not her stiffening fingers or boxy outdated machine. She never expected results. Her life was one of infinite patience and unfinished business, an existence of relations drawn out.

Quick she didn't look for either. The only quick she had known was her shiddach. One flit of a date in the lobby of a Manhattan hotel and the next month married. For that bit of economy she had paid with eighteen years of miserable marriage and eighteen years separated, waiting for Berel to give her a divorce. She was Royal Hills's agunah, their woman in waiting—trapped in Jewish marriage by loopholeless laws. Not to think that New York State did for her better. A state with no no-fault divorce. Even the blessing of the gentile court she couldn't get. Her reasons weren't prima facie. The judge was not impressed. What more should she have to say than she didn't want to be married? Idiot rules. No-fault in itself an

idiot concept. Anyone who's experienced will tell you the
same: when a marriage fails, always, always there is fault.

Up on the stool, switches flicked, the circular bulb of the magnifying light crackled while the gases fired up and raced round
the tube. Lili pushed the light into place—Gitta's halo. She
then witch-hazeled the glass center, witch-hazeled the needle,
witch-hazeled Gitta, and leaned in.

"I went to the kabbalist," Gitta said, "went to the rabbi.
Useless both."

"And who said useless from the start?"

"Still, I thought," Gitta said. "Better to try the others one
more time. Mystical numbers, I brought. A kabbalist's feast.
Married at eighteen for eighteen years. And now eighteen
years waiting for a divorce. One second it took to explain.
Clear as I'm telling you."

"Easy numbers," Lili agreed.

"I got the same as they've been giving all along," Gitta said.
"The rabbi wanting to know if there was someone else, if I'd
fallen in love, if, God forbid, I was pregnant. The kabbalist, no
better. A blessing at the end, much mazal and a healed marriage and a house full of children. Fifty-four years old and
wishing me children. And me with a hot flash in the middle."

"They're waiting for Berel to die of old age. They'll bring
you a divorce when they can trail in the mud off his grave
along with it. Enough is enough. If he needs to die for you to
live, then see to it yourself." For emphasis, Lili sank in the
needle and hit the pedal twice, shock-shocking Gitta and
tweezing out the freed hair.

"I picture it done, sometimes. Berel face-down behind the
supermarket drowned in a puddle, or in his apartment with a
broken neck, by a broken ladder, an empty fixture hanging
from the ceiling, and a lightbulb broken in his hand. Acci-

dents. Who would guess? No trail from him to me, from me to you, from you to a husband with a cousin who knows people who do such things."

"It's a simple transaction, Gitta. Berel's life spent to buy back yours. At this point, a fair price to pay."

"Terrible. Terrible talk. There is still the matchmaker. A saner idea."

"Who's been saying matchmaker from the start? You want business done, do it in a business way. You don't go looking for some rabbi's sympathy, you go to the source. If this guy made the match, let him undo it, and let him know there are more permanent solutions. Trust me, it's not killing but the prospect of killing that gets things done."

"And if it doesn't?"

"Then there is killing. Win-win situation. For once. For Gitta. Win-win."

Looking at her now, Liebman remembered her then. He was a pious man and not one for staring. But the matchmaker, well, he is part of a highly specialized field, like the doctor. He is forced to look, to see, with honest eyes.

His memory confirmed what he saw before him: a woman not easy to match.

This was not just a cruel judgment, not because so maybe one of her eyes was a little higher than the other, and one of her breasts a whole lot lower so that it pointed out and down and looked like it was embarrassed on its own about the condition and trying to sneak behind Gitta's back to hide. It had nothing even to do with her trademark hirsuteness.

What Little Liebman could not afford to ignore was her nature. A generous person might pretend not to notice. But it's the matchmaker's job to know. Gitta Floog had always been different, and it threatened everyone. And for all the unfairness she'd seen in her life, Royal Hills somehow looked upon her thankfully. A sad case, but always someone has to suffer. Better it was Gitta. Somehow, underneath, they thought it. Gitta got what she deserved.

For this prevailing, unspoken feeling, Liebman felt worst of all. In thirty-six years of successful matchmaking she was his only agunah. And to his only agunah he owed his success.

Little Liebman had long trailed Heshel the Matchmaker begging a chance to make a match on his own. Drinking tea one afternoon with all the big machers, Heshel had called Liebman over, thought it would be funny to give his mascot a shot.

Slurping at his tea, biting through a sugar cube clamped between rotten teeth, Heshel pulled Liebman onto his knee. "Shmegegge," he said, "I've got a job for you. The Floog girl needs a man." And in the way matchmakers joke privately, he added, "The time has come to cut off her braids and trim down that beard."

Liebman skulked off. He did not kid himself about the task. At a more delicate age Liebman's own father used to slap him on the back of the head and tell him to drink some milk, to learn some more Torah. "Not a hair on you and already the girls in your grade have mustaches like they've learned the Gemara once through."

To everyone's surprise, Liebman had married her off—and in one date, yet. Parents began sleeping better, no longer worrying over the boy with the short leg, the girl with the port stain, and, worse, the children with selfishness and anger etched in their eyes. Liebman's business was airborne. For a short while, until the neighbors whispered about the noise from the newlyweds' apartment and the loveless look to the husband and his head-hung wife, it was true glory for the new matchmaker.

Gitta had long since become his shame. It was bad for business to have her standing there with arms crossed and tapping a foot, Gitta Floog on display in front of his dining room window. Liebman sighed. He waved her forward, rushed her down a hallway. Gitta expected no less. She followed him into a back office with a ratty couch and a file cabinet, a dingy room off the alley.

This is how Little Liebman the matchmaker found himself alone with Gitta Floog trying to convince him to undo what he'd done.

"Forty years ago, Gitta. My very first match."

"Why me for practice? Why my life sacrificed to get started yours?" She dropped down onto the crumpled sheet spread over the sofa.

"A good rate, Gitta. Even for a first match. Even for then. A symbolic commission, I took, if ever there was." He did not say what he was thinking, did not mention the miracle he had performed. Nothing nice to say so he said what he could. "Forty years is late for a customer to come back."

"Thirty-six, first of all. Eighteen married, eighteen waiting for Berel to break."

"So thirty-six. Still a long time for the customer to return."

Gitta stood up, moved close to Liebman. She looked down into his eyes.

"A hammer," she said. "At Sears they will replace a hammer for life."

"This is because of volume, Gitta. Where there is volume people can afford."

"So I'll pay," she said. "Same as a match. I'll pay you to unmake a wedding, same as to do."

Her eye swims over the glass, swells and softens, runs suddenly long. Then precision focus and Lili's steady gaze. This is how Gitta knows her, through snippets of clarity and a collection of ever-warping parts, her view from the underside of the magnifying light. Gitta was thinking about this and ignoring Lili's diatribe, when Lili said, "Stubborn hair," and turned up the power on the machine.

"What do you mean, he doesn't want to get involved? We have involved him already. The day he introduced you to Berel he involved himself. Tell him that, Gitta. Tell him when Berel shows up dead, he'll have no trouble understanding he's in."

"I can't do any of this."

"Then plan B. Gennaro?" Lili screamed to her husband. "Gennaro, get over here." They heard his footsteps as he approached the curtain that split the rest of the room from the salon.

"What?" he said through the fabric.

Gitta propped herself up on her elbows. "Do not, Lili. Do not start this yet. Not as a joke, not as a threat. Because I really might want it. If we do it, we do it for real."

"What?" Gennaro said.

"Put on the rice. Go put on the rice for dinner." They were silent while he walked off. Then Lili whispered, "You go explain to that midget. You go tell the matchmaker that he better beat a divorce out of your husband before you make the problem disappear. Tell him whatever you need to tell him, Widow Floog. Because you've got three choices. The matchmaker, Gennaro's cousin, or shutting your mouth. If you're never going to do anything, then save us both some energy. At least keep your mouth shut so I can do my work."

Lili guided the needle. "Back to the matchmaker," she said, and she pressed the pedal and held it down until Gitta thought she saw smoke.

. . .

Knocking did not bring him so Gitta looked round the alley for something with heft. Next to a Dumpster she found a pipe with a joint on the end and tested its weight. This she swung against the metal door at the back of the matchmaker's apartment. Each blow left a dent and made a noise that carried. She raised the pipe for a third swing when Liebman peered through the grimy window and then opened the door to the back room. He had an arm raised. Gitta was a large woman, and even a small foe with such a weapon—well, he would not put anything past her. The old suspicion.

"Put that thing down." Liebman cowered. "I've got a front door, too, you already know."

"Not trying to complicate," Gitta said. "Not trying to make extra trouble for you. You hide me in the back room, I'll keep myself hidden. I'm interested only in finishing our business."

"Business we don't have. You want your money back you can have it. I admit your match was no success."

Gitta dropped the pipe, pushed past Liebman, and made her way to the crumpled sheet on the ratty couch.

Liebman wrung his hands. "I can't help you," he said. "What could you be back for but to hear it again?"

"Do you know what my life is?" she said. "Do you know how it is?"

Liebman thought about this. He sort of did, he thought. He kind of knew. She was trapped. She was a woman anchored to a foul husband, a married widow or maybe a divorced wife. He was also aware of the superstition that surrounded her, mothers stepping between Gitta's crooked gaze and their newlywed daughters. She was a woman who raised whispers. Yes, he thought he understood.

"I know they talk about you," he said, "that all this time and they still talk."

"You think I don't hear the nonsense." Gitta turned red.

"They treat me like a witch. They say Berel snapped, chased me around the house with a razor, and kicked me out in a rage. They say I made a deal with the devil and was suddenly free of hair and husband—but like any devil deal it went horribly wrong." She covered her mouth. "I got rid of it to be pretty. The day I left. Got rid of it to maybe meet a new husband, have a child or two, and start a nice life."

"And?"

And what should she tell him, that Berel had won if winning meant ruining her life and losing meant seeing her happy and free?

Gitta told him what she needed to see the job done: "Maybe it *is* late, Liebman, maybe, you think, sad. But I'm here to tell you"—she smoothed her skirt, looked away— "Gitta Floog has fallen in love."

"Can't be," Liebman said, so surprised he didn't consider the insult involved.

"A shock, I'm sure. But such things happen on their own. Even to me. I'm in love, Liebman. And like our mother Sarah, even the greater wonder, I'm pregnant. When my period did not come, I thought it had gone, but fifty-four years old and I discover it's otherwise."

"Not Berel's?" was all Liebman could say. The scandal!

"A genius you are, Liebman. A detective. No, it's not Berel's. But the father is in our community, a hot-tempered man." She went on, though Liebman looked as though he might die. "We won't have our baby born a bastard."

"Then there really is a man?"

"Modern times, Liebman. Modern times. Still, in some form or another there's generally a man. Listen to me, he has found someone from outside, someone to make me a widow. Berel would be dead already if I hadn't begged a chance to talk with you. My companion is already decided. 'On Liebman's head' is what he told me. 'The whole mess, it's butter sitting on Liebman's head. Only Little Liebman can keep it from melting into his eyes.' "

"Who is he?" Liebman buttoned and unbuttoned his collar.

"When it's done, you'll know. You'll be the first invited to the wedding. Right now, though, it's time for violence. Only two facts that concern you. We'll kill him and I'm pregnant. So take your pick. Take your pick for what's more urgent. Take your pick for why it needs to get done. But the butter sits on your head, softening already."

Not long after Gitta stepped out of the alley, looked both ways, and crossed the street, a new rumor about Gitta Floog began to spread. Maybe it was someone who looked down from a narrow bathroom window with the banging of the pipe, or the sometimes homeless Akiva peering out from a Dumpster when the back door closed. Any number of people might have seen Gitta step out of Liebman's alley into the bright light of day. But the base of the rumor, the meat of it, well, only one person, only Little Liebman, could be guilty of letting it slip.

Proportion was the first thing to go. Even before the rumor had reached proper dispatch it ballooned past belief and had to be scaled back to an absorbable size. There were stylistic variations, of course, but one detail stuck, providing the rumor with unassailable authenticity. It was the addition of Liebman's name as father of the child and Gitta's secret man. It was a twist Liebman hadn't thought of, an advantage of which Gitta hadn't dreamed.

From that instant on, no one needed it over more than Liebman. What parent would trust a matchmaker caught up in a scandal? How to let him judge a prospective son-in-law's character if he can't seem to manage his own? No, the deal was done. Liebman was fully involved.

11

Three windows faced the street in Gitta's efficiency. The one over the dormant radiator was open a crack. On the other side of the long room was a kitchen area, the front door, and a panel with the buzzer in between.

It was after the first beating, and Gitta sat in a chair in the center of her apartment. This was the best she could do.

Berel was screaming outside. His voice carried up the three stories and made its way through the crack in the window. It was a terrible effect. Gitta's blinds were drawn, and the voice, localized and harsh, taunted her from that corner, as if Berel were somehow floating outside her window and yelling in. Then he'd pause—a second's silence—and the buzzer would start screeching on her other side. Again, this sense of his presence, Berel standing in the hallway leaning on a button right outside the door.

She had no television and no radio. She couldn't concentrate on her reading or the Psalms. So she had pulled a chair to the middle of the room as far as she could get from Berel on both sides.

And she sat there, head in her hands, trapped between him.

Lili flicked the switch on her machine and hit the side panel until the power light glowed.

Gitta was spread out on the table.

"Repetitive nightmares like my father used to have about Siberia. Sometimes Berel comes through the window and sometimes through the door. It's an elopement. Berel is in a suit. I'm gowned and veiled and clutching a bouquet. Every night he carries me away, either by the door or down a ladder, always with the flowers in my arms. And always, whether from their windows or lining the hallway, the neighbors are watching and wishing us luck. From the outside it looks like perfect romance. And I can see why they confuse the bride's weak moaning—all of them smiling and waving at my call for help. They stand there cooing while Berel rips my dress off, tears it all off right there in front of them, everything but the veil."

"Under the veil?" Lili wants to know. "What's under the veil?"

"Hairless," Gitta says. "No prettier or uglier and can't tell you my age. But hairless, hairless I am sure."

Lili smiles at that, goes after a stray follicle between Gitta's eyebrows, lands the needle, strikes a nerve so that Gitta's left lid flutters and she feels a strange comfort, as if her face has been split appropriately and magically in two.

"He showed up again after the second beating, showed up out my window, buzzing at my door. This time he stayed longer. It was supposed to improve, Lili, but it's made my life only worse. Every bit of punishment he gets, he takes out on me tenfold. Hard-hearted, my Berel. That's what the matchmaker says. He keeps calling to tell me Berel will never give in."

"And what do you say?"

"I say exactly as we practiced: 'There are two ways to free an agunah. One is for the husband to give a get. And the other, to bring proof of his death. One way or the other, Liebman. One way or the other.'"

"Oh, that's good, Gitta. That last 'one way' is very good."

Berel was returning from a night trip to the supermarket. One moment he was walking and the next in a car with four other men—his groceries left spilled on the sidewalk.

The men wore children's plastic masks with tight swirls of yellow hair and red, red lips, little Queen Esther masks on each one. But the disguises did not sufficiently cover their grown-up faces. Black beards burst out from behind bulbous rouged cheeks. Sidelocks stuck out like pigtails from under elastic bands.

They punched Berel and smacked him before anyone said a word.

Then the one in the front passenger seat, the smallest by far, turned to talk to Berel, restrained between two Esthers in the back.

"Hard to find people willing to beat you anymore, Berel. Not out of mercy, but because it's become such a chore."

"Such a tiny, tiny thug," Berel said, "I was wondering. And then the familiar voice. Since when are you so bold, Little Liebman, as to place yourself at the scene of the crime?"

"Maybe this time I don't leave anyone to talk."

Little Liebman motioned to the two Esthers and they wrestled Berel onto his stomach and taped his hands to his ankles so that they might carry him like a bundle. The one on the right unlocked his door. "This ride," Liebman said, "I'm making it clear. Tonight we make progress."

"You want progress, Liebman? I've got some of my own. As soon as you let me loose, I'm headed straight for the newspapers. I'm going to tip the goyim off to the injustice that goes on."

"The newspapers?" Liebman laughed. "Yes, have them report it. Just the kind of Jewish story the papers love."

"It will ruin you, Liebman."

"If only you heard the rumors. My name is already ruined. Let them run it on the front page. In New York you'll find no sympathy for a man who enslaves his wife. The feminists will bring me a medal for beating you. The mayor will put me on a float in the Thanksgiving Day parade."

The car headed out on the highway, a change in rhythm. Every few seconds a seam in the road so that the smoothness of speed was broken, the constancy interrupted by a rhythmic *thuck*.

The car door by his head opened and Berel was lowered toward the flowing script of road. He worried not over disfigurement but loss of senses, being rubbed clean of eyes or tongue, being rolled into the alley without his ears. Berel screamed into the wind and was pulled back in.

"Now give the get or we head out to drown you at Jones Beach. Two to hold you under the water and two kosher witnesses to watch."

"You won't do it," Berel said. "You're a matchmaker, not a murderer. You understand the sanctity of unions. Like in nature, Liebman. Like it says about pigeons. You kill one, you have to kill its mate. To make it kosher you've got to kill both, me and Gitta both."

Berel was once again lowered. Dangerously close. A pebble shot from a tire hit Berel in the cheek. He moved his tongue to try and find it in his mouth, sure the stone had cut through. They lifted him back in.

"With arranged marriages," Liebman said, "a good match is as difficult as separating the earth from the sky. Don't you think? A wonder they ever hold."

Berel buried his face in the warmth of the right-hand Esther's lap.

"Gitta is desperate, Berel. Desperate. At this point she feels it's your life or hers. And we can't have another generation ruined by this marriage. Royal Hills doesn't need another mamzer. No, we cannot have a bastard born because of you."

"A bastard?" This was too much. "If she's pregnant, I'll tear it from her womb." Berel went mad, fought like a tiger, put on quite a show for a man with arms and legs tied behind his back. There was a struggle to control him. They slammed Berel's head against the door until Liebman screamed for them to stop. He thought they might knock the life from the body, as if the soul were a filling to be loosed from a tooth.

"Are you still with us, Berel?" Leibman held on to the back of his seat.

Berel nodded, licking his lips.

"Any chance you're thinking clearly now? Might you reconsider before we kill you?"

"That's what you'll have to do," Berel said, perking up. "Like in the American ceremony. Till death do us part."

Liebman pulled off his mask and rubbed at his eyes. He nodded to the men.

This time when Berel was lowered out the door he felt the car speed up and the grip tighten on his hair. The one with his legs used maximum control. And like artisans attending to that final detail, Berel's head was forced to the grindstone, his face to the road. For an instant. For a touch. The Esthers took off a perfect circle, a sliver—not deep—of Berel's nose.

Berel screamed outside her window, taunts and threats, declarations of a love he'd never shown. And his refrain, "Why do they beat me?" This—as if he couldn't come up with a reason—he yelled again and again.

Gitta had things she would have liked to scream. She'd have liked to stand under the window of every Jew in Royal Hills and scream at the top of her lungs, demand to know why her divorce needs an excuse or a consent, anyone's help at all.

After Berel left, Gitta carried her chair back to the table, put on a sweater, and wandered over to the bridge. She followed the walkway, gazing out at the river, the traffic speeding by on her other side. This was the old decision Gitta had pondered. Not life or death for Berel, but traffic or river, traffic or water, to which side should she dive?

Little Liebman handed Gitta an apple and leaned against the file cabinet. "Showing already," he said, looking at her stomach.

She stared back at him, the corners of her mouth turned

down. She didn't appreciate the familiarity and didn't trust Liebman's invitation. It was the first time he'd asked her over since the beatings began.

"Every nightmare has its end, Gitta. Berel has come to his senses."

"Nonsense. What, he promised a divorce while you twisted an arm? He came to my house after, same as always. Floated outside my window screaming in my ear." Gitta lowered herself onto the couch as if she were indeed carrying extra weight. She sniffed at the apple. "When he throws the get in my face, Little Liebman, then I'll know it's done."

"We put a fear into him and he wouldn't budge. We dumped him in the alley half dead and still swearing he'd never see you free. Then three days ago he shows up here, then yesterday, and again this morning. Each time more remorseful, each time clearer in what he had to say. It's the little mamzer that got him," Liebman pointed at his belly. "Not for you or himself does he have any mercy, but only for the unborn. The suffering of the father, he said, should not be borne out on the son."

"Suddenly there is sense?"

"He's never lied before. Stubborn and coconut brained, he runs around spouting nonsense. But never has he agreed falsely to a divorce. He too, like you, thinks there is some trick. He says meet him once and tell him to his face that you carry another man's child. He doesn't ask for the man's name. He doesn't want to hear a tiny heartbeat or see a note from a doctor. He says, after the degradation of how he learned, he will only bring you a divorce if you tell him about the baby yourself."

Lili bent a needle. She put down the wand and fished around for a replacement, talking all the while and working herself into a rage.

"Eighteen years it takes you to build up the courage and then you buy into nonsense like this. I'm coming with you, Gitta. I'm going to strangle that bum myself."

"The matchmaker is right. Berel's never lied."

Lili slid the magnifying light out of the way and moved her face right to Gitta's so that crooked eyes crossed.

"You're meeting in a hotel, fine, perfect. But let me tell you something, Berel's not offering you a divorce, Gitta, he's offering an alibi. Why not have it so, when he leaves, a gypsy cab jumps the curb and runs him down? You can be the first to scream, to yell in a lobby with one hundred witnesses, while Berel is hit-and-runned right outside."

"I lived with him for too long not to know what goes on in that miserable mind. Berel is finally tired. He is going to give me my divorce. Soon I'll have my life back and then who knows what I'll do? Get to work on those roots, Lili. I might yet find romance."

Yes, she is bitter. Her second date in fifty-four years and again with Berel. Again in the lobby of a Manhattan hotel. Her corpse will rot, she is sure, without ever having anyone hold open a door.

Gitta stepped down the three stairs into the deep, narrow lobby, chose a couch and a chair unoccupied by any of the long-legged, knife-chinned men and women—so smartly dressed and fortified.

Before she had sunk fully into the chair a waitress approached. Gitta ordered a crème de menthe which she would not touch. Her way of paying rent for sitting.

Over the years, Gitta had crossed the street more than once to avoid Berel, hurried into the women's section or out a side door to escape a confrontation at shul. This wasn't the first time she'd laid eyes on him since, but as he made his way down those three steps, her only lover in a lifetime, her husband and tormentor, she realized that she'd not uttered a word to him since she'd left.

He'd gotten old. His beard was full of white and his cheeks hung loose on his skull. And then there were the bruises. She could see the blood-black of one under his beard and the more shocking perfect scab on the end of his nose.

"I came to ask you," he said, in a voice detached, as if sending a message with this Gitta to take back to his wife, "if you'll give me the child."

Gitta chewed at her bottom lip, lowered her chin. Despicable from the start.

"Not this way," Gitta said. "I say what you want to hear and you give me what's left of my life."

"I'm allowed to ask, no? Denied so many things, you couldn't expect I wouldn't ask." He was sad, suddenly. She could see. Amazing. How many crimes produce only victims, Gitta wondered, everyone claiming innocence and everyone hurt.

The waitress put down a napkin and set a glass in front of Gitta.

"You've fallen so low that you eat in a trayf hotel? So adultery is not your only sin?"

"It's only a drink, Berel, and I've yet to touch it. And what I do is none of your business. I want from you only one thing."

"And I wanted from you only one thing. The duties of a wife fulfilled." He did not change his tone, but the old, loose skin began to tighten, his rage, as from an organ ruptured, began to seep into cheeks and purple tongue, spread through the broken veins of his nose. "All I wanted. To see my name live on."

"Wasted energy, Berel. You hear me say it and then you give me a divorce. Agreed? Just as you told Liebman."

Berel snorted at that.

"What is my word to Liebman who beats and degrades me and is said to be the father of your bastard child?"

"What is this, Berel? This is not what was planned."

"No, neither did I plan a life of misery because of you. I was about to give you a divorce, you should know. Thought it out, talked to my rebbe, I was literally on my way over to arrange it the first time they pulled me into that car. Later, even with those Nazis hounding me, I saw it was time to give in. Then Liebman told me you were pregnant."

How he knew her, understood how to tear her in half, not Lili's peaceful, electric-needle magic, but how to tear her whole being apart, rip her brutally in two.

"You weren't ever going to give anything," she said. "This is another of your tortures."

"Shaming me, making me a shame in my community, and you talk of torture. What does a whore need a divorce for when she sells herself either way?"

Gitta went hot with panic. Her recurring reality was as bad as her nightmares. It was supposed to improve. Somehow, sometime, her life was supposed to get better. She grabbed at Berel's sleeve and pulled him close.

"There is no baby," she said. "My own trick. I've been loyal all these years." Gitta tried for a smile but got tears. "Now you must," and she was crying, "must," and she was yelling, "must give me a divorce before I die."

"I only came for the truth," he said. And like that he was up, shaking her hand free, and taking the three stairs in a stride.

Gitta stood and watched Berel push his way round the revolving door, saw a handsome young man pop out in his place.

She tried to imagine the high-pitched screech of brakes, the car hitting and thumping, the gypsy cab racing off into the night. Gitta could call Lili from a phone booth and see it over with before morning. She could wake up knowing he was gone and say her prayers with fervor. Because she could take it, she could live with his murder.

Gitta unzipped her wallet and shook her head.

How close he comes, her Berel. His whole life a near-death experience, teetering on the blade of her courage.

She thought too of Liebman, who said he knew, he felt, suffered right there along with her. Even when she makes a denial, even when no baby comes, he will still be tied to the rumors. Royal Hills would make it fit, with an adoption, a miscarriage, a hairy dwarf child not well and locked away. Let him know from it, she felt. She did not feel generous. Did not at all care.

Then Gitta thought of herself, the years remaining, the end of this life. Let it be short, she thought. Though she knew she would see a hundred and twenty years. It would be like in the old wives' tales, corpses laid to rest still growing thick, yellow nails and wiry hair. And this Gitta knew, folktale or not, would be her doom—buried, waiting, the wrong man's ring going loose around her finger, and a scholar's beard growing and growing. Roots buried deeper than even Lili had dreamed. Hair growing from bone.

For the Relief
of Unbearable Urges

The beds were to be separated on nights forbidden to physical intimacy, but Chava Bayla hadn't pushed them together for many months. She flatly refused to sleep anywhere except on her menstrual bed and was, from the start, impervious to her husband's pleading.

"You are pure," Dov Binyamin said to the back of his wife, who—heightening his frustration—slept facing the wall.

"I am impure."

"This is not true, Chava Bayla. It's an impossibility. And I know myself the last time you went to the ritual bath. A woman does not have her thing—"

"Her thing?" Chava said. She laughed, as if she had caught him in a lie, and turned to face the room.

"A woman doesn't menstruate for so long without even a single week of clean days. And a wife does not for so long ignore her husband. It is Shabbos, a double mitzvah tonight—an obligation to make love."

Chava Bayla turned back again to face her wall. She tightened her arms around herself as if in an embrace.

"You are my wife!" Dov Binyamin said.

"That was God's choice, not mine. I might also have been put on this earth as a bar of soap or a kugel. Better," she said, "better it should have been one of those."

That night Dov Binyamin slept curled up on the edge of his bed—as close as he could get to his wife.

After Shabbos, Chava avoided coming into the bedroom for as long as possible. When she finally did enter and found Dov dozing in a chair by the balcony, she went to sleep fully clothed, her sheitel still on top of her head.

As he nodded forward in the chair, Dov's hat fell to the floor. He woke up, saw his wife, picked up his hat, and, brushing away the dust with his elbow, placed it on the nightstand. How beautiful she looked all curled up in her dress. Like a princess enchanted, he thought. Dov pulled the sheet off the top of his bed. He wanted to cover her, to tuck Chava in. Instead he flung the sheet into a corner. He shut off the light, untied his shoes—but did not remove them—and went to sleep on the tile floor beside his wife's bed. Using his arm for a pillow, Dov Binyamin dreamed of a lemon ice his uncle had bought him as a child and of the sound of the airplanes flying overhead at the start of the Yom Kippur War.

Dov Binyamin didn't go to work on Sunday. Folding up his tallis after prayers and fingering the embroidery of the tallis bag, he recalled the day Chava had presented it to him as a wedding gift—the same gift his father had received from his mother, and his father's father before. Dov had marveled at the workmanship, wondered how many hours she had spent with a needle in hand. Now he wondered if she would ever find him worthy of such attentions again. Zipping the prayer shawl inside, Dov Binyamin put the bag under his arm. He carried it with him out of the shul, though he had his own cubby in which to store it.

The morning was oppressively hot; a hamsin was settling over Jerusalem. Dov Binyamin was wearing his lightest caftan, but in the heat wave it felt as if it were made of the heaviest wool.

Passing a bank of phones, he considered calling work, making some excuse, or even telling the truth. "Shai," he would say, "I am a ghost in my home and wonder who will mend my tallis bag when it is worn." His phone card was in his wallet, which he had forgotten on the dresser, and what did he want to explain to Shai for, who had just come from a Shabbos with his spicy wife and a house full of children.

Dov followed Jaffa Street down to the Old City. Roaming the alleyways always helped to calm him. There was comfort in the Jerusalem stone and the walls within walls and the permanence of everything around him. He felt a kinship with history's Jerusalemites, in whose struggles he searched for answers to his own. Lately he felt closer to his biblical heroes than to the people with whom he spent his days. King David's desires were far more alive to Dov than the empty problems of Shai and the other men at the furniture store.

Weaving through the Jewish Quarter, he had intended to end up at the Wall, to say Tehillim, and, in his desperate state, to scribble a note and stuff it into a crack just like the tourists in their cardboard yarmulkes. Instead, he found himself caught up in the crush inside the Damascus Gate. An old Arab woman was crouched down behind a wooden box of cactus fruit. She peeled a sabra with a kitchen knife, allowing a small boy a sample of her product. The child ran off with his mouth open, a stray thorn stuck in his tongue.

Dov Binyamin tightened his hold on the tallis bag and pushed his way through the crowd. He walked back to Mea Shearim along the streets of East Jerusalem. Let them throw stones, he thought. Though no one did. No one even took notice of him except to step out of his way as he rushed to his rebbe's house for some advice.

Meir the Beadle was in the front room, sitting on a plastic chair at a plastic table.

"Don't you have work today?" Meir said, without looking up from the papers that he was shifting from pile to pile.

Dov Binyamin ignored the question. "Is the Rebbe in?"

"He's very busy."

Dov Binyamin went over to the kettle, poured himself a mug of hot water, and stirred in a spoonful of Nescafé. "How about you don't give me a hard time today?"

"Who's giving a hard time?" Meir said, putting down the papers and getting up from the chair. "I'm just telling you Sunday is busy after a day and a half without work." He knocked at the Rebbe's door and went in. Dov Binyamin made a blessing over his coffee, took a sip, and, being careful not to spill, lowered himself into one of the plastic chairs. The coffee cut the edge off the heat that, like Dov, sat heavy in the room.

The Rebbe leaned forward on his shtender and rocked back and forth as if he were about to topple.

"No, this is no good. Very bad. Not good at all." He pulled back on the lectern and held it in that position. The motion reminded Dov of his dream, of the rumbling of engines and a vase—there had been a blue glass vase—set to rocking on a shelf. "And you don't want a divorce?"

"I love her, Rebbe. She is my wife."

"And Chava Bayla?"

"She, thank God, has not even raised the subject of separation. She asks nothing of me but to be left alone. And this is where the serpent begins to swallow its tail. The more she rejects me, the more I want to be with her. And the more I want to be with her, the more intent she becomes that I stay away."

"She is testing you."

"Yes. In some way, Rebbe, Chava Bayla is giving to me a test."

Pulling at his beard, the Rebbe again put his full weight on the lectern so that the wood creaked. He spoke in a Talmudic singsong:

"Then you must find the strength to ignore Chava Bayla, until Chava Bayla should come to find you—and you must be strict with yourself. For she will not consider your virtues until she is calm in the knowledge that her choices are her own."

"But I don't have the strength. She is my wife. I miss her. And I am human, too. With human habits. It will be impossible for me not to try and touch her, to try and convince her. Rebbe, forgive me, but God created the world with a certain order to it. I suffer greatly under the urges with which I have been blessed."

"I see," said the Rebbe. "The urges have become great."

"Unbearable. And to be around someone that I feel so strongly for, to look and be unable to touch—it is like floating through heaven in a bubble of hell."

The Rebbe pulled a chair over to the bookcases that lined his walls. Climbing onto the chair, he steadied himself, then removed a volume from the top shelf. "We must relieve the pressure."

"It is a fine notion. But I fear that it's impossible."

"I'm giving you a heter," the Rebbe said. "A special dispensation." He went over to his desk and flipped through the book. He began to scribble on a pad of onionskin paper.

"For what?"

"To see a prostitute."

"Excuse me, Rebbe?"

"Your marriage is at stake, is it not?"

Dov bit at his thumbnail and then rushed the hand, as if it were something shameful, into the pocket of his caftan.

"Yes," he said, a shake entering his voice. "My marriage is a withered limb at my side."

The Rebbe aimed his pencil at Dov.

"One may go to great lengths in the name of achieving peace in the home."

"But a prostitute?" Dov Binyamin asked.

"For the relief of unbearable urges," the Rebbe said. And he tore, like a doctor, the sheet of paper from the pad.

Dov Binyamin drove to Tel Aviv, the city of sin. There he was convinced he would find plenty of prostitutes. He parked his Fiat on a side street off Dizengoff and walked around town.

Though he was familiar with the city, its social aspects were foreign to him. It was the first leisurely walk he had taken in Tel Aviv and, fancying himself an anthropologist in a foreign land, he found it all quite interesting. He was usually the one under scrutiny. Busloads of American tourists scamper through Mea Shearim daily. They buy up the stores and pull tiny cameras from their hip packs, snapping pictures of real live Hasidim, like the ones from the stories their grandparents told. Next time he would say "Boo!" He laughed at the thought of it. Already he was feeling lighter. Passing a kiosk, he stopped and bought a bag of pizza-flavored Bissli. When he reached the fountain, he sat down on a bench among the aged new immigrants. They clustered together as if huddled against a biting cold wind that had followed them from their native lands. He stayed there until dark, until the crowd of new immigrants, like the bud of a flower, began to spread out, to open up, as the old folks filed down the fountain's ramps onto the city streets. They were replaced by young couples and groups of boys and girls who talked to each other from a distance but did not mix. So much like religious children, he thought. In a way we are all the same. Dov Binyamin suddenly felt overwhelmed. He was startled to find himself in Tel Aviv, already involved in the act of searching out a harlot, instead of home in his chair by the balcony, worrying over whether to take the Rebbe's advice at all.

He walked back toward his car. A lone cabdriver leaned up against the front door of his Mercedes, smoking. Dov Binyamin approached him, the heat of his feet inside his shoes becoming more oppressive with every step.

"Forgive me," Dov Binyamin said.

The cabdriver, his chest hair sticking out of the collar of his T-shirt in tufts, ground out the cigarette and opened the passenger door. "Need a ride, Rabbi?"

"I'm not a rabbi."

"And you don't need a ride?"

Dov Binyamin adjusted his hat. "No. Actually no."

The cabdriver lit another cigarette, flourishing his Zippo impressively. Dov took notice, though he was not especially impressed.

"I'm looking for a prostitute."

The cabdriver coughed and clasped a hand to his chest.

"Do I look like a prostitute?"

"No, you misunderstand." Dov Binyamin wondered if he should turn and run away. "A female prostitute."

"What's her name?"

"No name. Any name. You are a taxi driver. You must know where are such women." The taxi driver slapped the hood of his car and said, "Ha," which Dov took to be laughter. Another cab pulled up on Dov's other side.

"What's happening?" the second driver called.

"Nothing. The rabbi here wants to know where to find a friend. Thinks it's a cabdriver's responsibility to direct him."

"Do we work for the Ministry of Tourism?" the second driver asked.

"I just thought," Dov Binyamin said. His voice was high and cracking. It seemed to elicit pity in the second driver.

"There's a cash machine back on Dizengoff."

"Prostitutes at the bank?" Dov Binyamin said.

"No, not at the bank. But the service isn't free." Dov blushed under his beard. "Up by the train station in Ramat Gan—at the row of bus stops."

"All those pretty ladies aren't waiting for the bus to Haifa." This from the first driver, who again slapped the hood of his car and said, "Ha!"

The first time past, he did not stop, driving by the women at high speed and taking the curves around the cement island so that his wheels screeched and he could smell the burning rubber. Dov Binyamin slowed down, trying to maintain control of himself and the car, afraid that he had already drawn too much attention his way. The steering wheel began to vibrate in Dov's shaking hands. The Rebbe had given him permission, had instructed him. Was not the Rebbe's heter valid? This is what Dov Binyamin told his hands, but they continued to tremble in protest.

On his second time past, a woman approached the passenger door. She wore a matching shirt and pants. The outfit clung tightly, and Dov could see the full form of her body. Such immodesty! She tapped at the window. Dov Binyamin reached over to roll it down. Flustered, he knocked the gearshift, and the car lurched forward. Applying the parking brake, he opened the window the rest of the way.

"Close your lights," she instructed him. "We don't need to be onstage out here."

"Sorry," he said, shutting off the lights. He was comforted by the error, not wanting the woman to think he was the kind of man who employed prostitutes on a regular basis.

"You interested in some action?"

"Me?"

"A shy one," she said. She leaned through the window, and

Dov Binyamin looked away from her large breasts. "Is this your first time? Don't worry. I'll be gentle. I know how to treat a black hat."

Dov Binyamin felt the full weight of what he was doing. He was giving a bad name to all Hasidim. It was a sin against God's name. The urge to drive off, to race back to Jerusalem and the silence of his wife, came over Dov Binyamin. He concentrated on his dispensation.

"What would you know from black hats?" he said.

"Plenty," she said. And then, leaning in farther, "Actually, you look familiar." Dov Binyamin seized up, only to begin shaking twice as hard. He shifted into first and gave the car some gas. The prostitute barely got clear of the window.

When it seemed as if he wouldn't find a suitable match, a strong-looking young woman stepped out of the darkness.

"Good evening," he said.

She did not answer or ask any questions or smile. She opened the passenger door and sat down.

"What do you think you're doing?"

"Saving you the trouble of driving around until the sun comes up." She was American. He could hear it. But she spoke beautiful Hebrew, sweet and strong as her step. Dov Binyamin turned on his headlights and again bumped the gearshift so that the car jumped.

"Settle down there, Tiger," she said. "The hard part's over. All the rest of the work is mine."

The room was in an unlicensed hostel. It had its own entrance. There was no furniture other than a double bed and three singles. The only lamp stood next to the door.

The prostitute sat on the big bed with her legs curled underneath her. She said her name was Devorah.

"Like the prophetess," Dov Binyamin said.

"Exactly," Devorah said. "But I can only see into the immediate future."

"Still, it is a rare gift with which to have been endowed." Dov shifted his weight from foot to foot. He stood next to the large bed unable to bring himself to bend his knees.

"Not really," she said. "All my clients already know what's in store."

She was fiery, this one. And their conversation served to warm up the parts of Dov the heat wave had not touched. The desire that had been building in Dov over the many months so filled his body that he was surprised his skin did not burst from the pressure. He tossed his hat onto the opposite single, hoping to appear at ease, as sure of himself as the hairy-chested cabdriver with his cigarettes. The hat landed brim side down. Dov's muscles twitched reflexively, though he did not flip it onto its crown.

"Wouldn't you rather make your living as a prophetess?" he asked.

"Of course. Prophesying's a piece of cake. You don't have to primp all day for it. And it's much easier on the back, no wear and tear. Better for *you,* too. At least you'd leave with something in the morning." She took out one of her earrings, then, as an afterthought, put it back in. "Doesn't matter anyway. No money in it. They pay me to do everything *except* look into the future."

"I'll be the first then," he said, starting to feel almost comfortable. "Tell me what you see."

She closed her eyes and tilted her head so that her lips began to part, this in the style of those who peer into other realms. "I predict that this is the first time you've done such a thing."

"That is not a prophecy. It's a guess." Dov Binyamin cleared his throat and wiggled his toes against the tops of his shoes. "What else do you predict?"

She massaged her temples and held back a naughty grin.
"That you will, for once, get properly laid."

But this was too much for Dov Binyamin. Boiling in the
heat and his shame, he motioned toward his hat.

Devorah took his hand.

"Forgive me," she said, "I didn't mean to be crude."

Her fingers were tan and thin, more delicate than Chava's.
How strange it was to see strange fingers against the whiteness
of his own.

"Excluding the affections of my mother, blessed be her
memory, this is the first time I have been touched by a woman
that is not my wife."

She released her grasp and, before he had time to step
away, reached out for him again, this time more firmly, as if
shaking on a deal. Devorah raised herself up and straightened
a leg, displayed it for a moment, and then let it dangle over the
side of the bed. Dov admired the leg, and the fingers resting
against his palm.

"Why are we here together?" she asked—she was not mocking him. Devorah pulled at the hand and he sat at her side.

"To relieve my unbearable urges. So that my wife will be
able to love me again."

Devorah raised her eyebrows and pursed her lips.

"You come to me for your wife's sake?"

"Yes."

"You are a very dedicated husband."

She gave him a smile that said, You won't go through with
it. The smile lingered, and then he saw that it said something
completely different, something irresistible. And he wondered, as a shiver ran from the trunk of his body out to the
hand she held, if what they say about American women is true.

Dov walked toward the door, not to leave, but to shut off
the lamp.

"One minute," Devorah said, reaching back and removing

a condom from a tiny pocket—no more than a slit in the smooth black fabric of her pants. Dov Binyamin knew what it was and waved it away.

"Am I really your second?" she asked.

Dov heard more in the question than was intended. He heard a flirtation; he heard a woman who treated the act of being second as if it were special. He was sad for her—wondering if she had ever been anyone's first. He did not answer out loud, but instead nodded, affirming.

Devorah pouted as she decided, the prophylactic held between two fingers like a quarter poised at the mouth of a jukebox. Dov switched off the light and took a half step toward the bed. He stroked at the darkness, moving forward until he found her hair, soft, alive, without any of the worked-over stiffness of Chava's wigs.

"My God," he said, snatching back his hand as if he had been stung. It was too late, though. That he already knew. The hunger had flooded his whole self. His heart was swollen with it, pumping so loudly and with such strength that it overpowered whatever sense he might have had. For whom then, he wondered, was he putting on, in darkness, such a bashful show? He reached out again and stroked her hair, shaking but sure of his intent. With his other arm, the weaker arm, to which he bound every morning his tefillin, the arm closer to the violent force of his heart, he searched for her hand.

Dov found it and took hold of it, first roughly, as if desperate. Then he held it lightly, delicately, as if it were made of blown glass—a goblet from which, with ceremony, he wished to drink. Bringing it toward his mouth, he began to speak.

"It is a sin to spill seed in vain," he said, and Devorah let the condom fall at the sound of his words.

Dov Binyamin was at work on Monday and he was home as usual on Monday night. There was no desire to slip out of the apartment during the long hours when he could not sleep, no temptation, when making a delivery in Ramot, to turn the car in the direction of Tel Aviv. Dov Binyamin felt, along with a guilt that he could not shake, a sense of relief. He knew that he could never be with another woman again. And if it were possible to heap on himself all the sexual urges of the past months, if he could undo the single night with the prostitute to restore his unadulterated fidelity, he would have them tenfold. From that night of indulgence he found the strength to wait a lifetime for Chava's attentions—if that need be.

When Chava Bayla entered the dining room, Dov Binyamin would move into the kitchen. When she entered the bedroom, he would close his eyes and feign sleep. He would lie in the dark and silently love his wife. And, never coming to a conclusion, he would rethink the wisdom of the Rebbe's advice. He would picture the hairy arm of the cabdriver as he slapped the hood of his taxi. And he would chide himself. Never, never would he accuse his wife of faking impurity, for was it not the greater sin for him to pretend to be pure?

It was only a number of days from that Sunday night that Chava Bayla began to talk to her husband with affection. Soon after, she touched him on the shoulder while handing him a platter of kasha varnishkes. He placed it on the table and ate in silence. As she served dessert, levelesh, his favorite, Dov's guilt took on a physical form. What else could it be? What else but guilt would strike a man so obviously?

It began as a concentrated smoldering that flushed the whole of his body. Quickly intensifying, it left him almost feverish. He would excuse himself from meals and sneak out of bed. At work, frightened and in ever-increasing pain, he ran from customers to examine himself in the bathroom. Dov Binyamin knew he was suffering from something more than shame.

But maybe it was a trial, a test of which the Rebbe had not warned him. For as his discomfort increased, so did Chava's attentions. On her way out of the shower, she let her towel drop in front of him, stepping away from it as if she hadn't noticed, like some Victorian woman waiting for a gentleman to return her hankie with a bow. She dressed slowly, self-consciously, omitting her undergarments and looking to Dov to remind her. He ignored it all, feeling the weight of his heart—no longer pumping as if to burst, but just as large—the blood stagnant and heavy. Chava began to linger in doorways so that he would be forced to brush against her as he passed. Her passion was torturous to Dov, forced to keep his own hidden inside. Once, without any of the protocol with which they tempered their lives, she came at the subject head-on. "Are you such a small man," she said, "that you must for eternity exact revenge?" He made no answer. It was she who walked away, only to return sweeter and bolder. She became so daring, so desperate, that he wondered if he had ever known the true nature of his wife at all. But he refused, even after repeated advances, to respond to Chava Bayla in bed.

She called to him from the darkness.

"Dovey, please, come out of there. Come lie by me and we'll talk. Just talk. Come Doveleh, join me in bed."

Dov Binyamin stood in the dark in the bathroom. There was some light from the street, enough to make out the toilet and the sink. He heard every word his wife said, and each one tore at him.

He stood before the toilet, holding his penis lightly, mindful of halacha and the laws concerning proper conduct in the lavatory. Trying to relieve himself, to pass water, he suffered to no end.

When he began to urinate, the burning worsened. He looked down in the half darkness and imagined he saw flames flickering from his penis.

He recalled the words of the prostitute. For his wife's sake, he thought, as the tears welled in his eyes. This couldn't possibly be the solution the Rebbe intended. Dov was supposed to be in his wife's embrace, enjoying her caresses, and instead he would get an examination table and a doctor's probing hands.

Dov Binyamin dropped to his knees. He rested his head against the coolness of the bowl. Whatever the trial, he couldn't bear it much longer. He had by now earned, he was sure, Chava Bayla's love.

There was a noise; it startled him; it was Chava at the door trying to open it. Dov had locked himself in. The handle turned again, and then Chava spoke to him through the door's frosted-glass window.

"Tell me," she said. "Tell me: When did I lose my husband for good?"

Every word a plague.

Dov pressed the lever of the toilet, drowning out Chava Bayla's voice. He let the tears run down his face and took his penis full in his hand.

For Dov Binyamin was on fire inside.

And yet he would not be consumed.

In This Way We Are Wise

Three blasts. Like birds. They come through the window, wild and lost. They are trapped under the high-domed ceiling of the café, darting round between us, striking walls and glass, knocking the dishes from the shelves. And we know, until they stop their terrible motion, until they cease swooping and darting and banging into the walls, until they alight, come to rest, exhausted, spent, there is nothing at all to do.

Plates in halves and triangles on the floor. A group of ceramic mugs, fat and split, like overripe fruit. The chandelier, a pendulum, still swings.

The owner, the waitress, the other few customers, sit. I am up at the windows. I am watching the people pour around the corner, watching them run toward us, mouths unhinged, pulling at hair, scratching at faces. They collapse and puff up, hop about undirected.

Like wild birds frightened.

Like people possessed, tearing at their forms trying to set something free.

Jerusalemites do not spook like horses. They do not fly like moths into the fire.

They have come to abide their climate. Terror as second winter, as part of their weather. Something that comes and then is gone.

. . .

Watching plumes of smoke, the low clouds of smoke that follow the people down the street, I suddenly need to be near the fire, to be where the ash still settles and café umbrellas burn.

I make for the door and the waitress stops me. The owner puts a hand on my shoulder.

"Calm down, Natan."

"Sit down, Natan."

"Have a coffee, Natan." The waitress is already on her way to the machine.

I feel an urgency the others dismiss. I can run with a child to a braking ambulance. Can help the barefooted find their shoes. The time, 3:16, my girlfriend late to meet me. I should be turning over bodies searching for her face.

In a chair drinking coffee holding the owner's hand. "There is nothing to do outside. No one to rescue. Who is already there is who's helping, Natan. If you are not in the eye when it happens, it's already too late to put yourself in."

I trade a picture of my girlfriend dead for one of her badly wounded.

Inbar with her face burned off, hands blown off, a leg severed near through. I will play the part of supportive one. I will bunch up and hold the sheet by her arm, smile and tell her how lucky she is to be alive and in a position where, having discussed it in a happy bed, in a lovers' bed, we had both sworn we'd rather die.

The phones are back. The streets secured. Soldiers everywhere, taking up posts and positions. Fingers curled by triggers.

An Arab worker comes out of the kitchen with a broom.

. . .

I'm the first to reach the phone, but I can't remember numbers. One woman slams a portable against the table, as if this will release the satellite from the army's grip.

I dial nonsense and hang up, unable to recollect even the code to my machine.

"Natan will be OK," I promise before leaving. "Natan is a grown man. He can find his way home."

On the street I am all animal. I am all sense, all smell and taste and touch. I can read every stranger's intentions from scent, from the flex of a muscle, the length of the passing of our eyes.

I'm on the corner and can turn up the block, take a few strides into the closest of kill zones. I can tour the stretch of wounded weeping and dead unmoving, walk past the blackened and burned, still smoldering ghosts.

The Hasidim will soon come to collect scattered bits, partial Christs. Parts of victims nailed up, screwed in, driven to stone and metal.

Hand pierced with rusted nail and hung on the base of a tree.

It is with true force, with the bit of higher thought I can muster, that I spare myself a lifetime of dreams.

I follow a street around and then back on the trail to Inbar's apartment.

She is there. We kiss and hug. She holds me in the doorway while I pass through the whole of evolution. The millions of years of animal knowing, of understanding without thought, subside.

We exchange stories of almosts, of near deaths, theories on fate and algorithm, probability and God. Inbar late, on a bus, distant thunder and then traffic. She got off with a few others and walked the rest of the way home.

She makes tea and we sit and watch our world on television.

There is the corner. There is a man reporting in front of my café. And then the long shot of the stretch I avoided. The street I walk on a dozen times a day. There is my cash machine, its awning shattered, its frame streaked with blood. There is the bazaar where I buy pens and pencils. The camera lingers over spilled notebooks, school supplies scattered, the implied contrast of death and a new school year. They will seek out distraught classmates, packs of crying girls, clutching girls, crawling-all-over-each-other-suckling-at-grief girls. They will get the boyfriends to talk, the parents to talk; they will have for us the complete drama, the house-to-house echo of all three blasts, before the week is through.

We watch our life on every channel. We turn to CNN for a top-of-the-hour translation of our world. Maybe English will make it more real.

It does not help. There is my café. There is my cash machine. There is the tree I wait by when there is waiting to be done.

"Would you recognize your own bedroom," I say, "if you saw it on TV?"

Inbar makes phone calls, receives phone calls, while I sit and watch the news. A constant cycle of the same story, little bits added each time. The phone calls remind me of America. The news, of America. Like snow days. Hovering around the radio in the morning. A chain list of calls. "Good morning, Mrs. Gold. It's Nathan speaking. Please tell Beth that school is closed because the buses can't come." The absurdity of the change. Years and miles. A different sort of weather. "Yes, hello Udi. It's Inbar. Another attack. Natan and I are fine."

. . .

Inbar tells me Israeli things, shares maxims on fate and luck. "We cannot live in fear," she says. "Of course you're terrified, it's terror after all." She has nonsensical statistics as well. "Five times more likely to be run over. Ten times more likely to die in a car. But you still cross the street don't you?"

She rubs my neck. Slips a hand under my shirt and rubs my back.

"Maybe I shouldn't," I say. A kiss on my ear. A switch of the channel. "Maybe it's time the street crossing stopped."

A biblical Israel, crowded with warriors and prophets, fallen kings and common men conscripted to do God's will. An American boy's Israel. A child raised up on causality and symbol.

Holocaust as wrath of God.

Israel the Phoenix rising up from the ashes.

The reporters trot out the odd survivors, the death defiers and nine lived. A girl with a small scratch on her cheek who stood two feet from the bomber, everyone around her dead. An old man with shrapnel buried in the hardcover book he was reading who survived the exact same way when the street blew up fifty years before. A clipping. He searches his wallet for a clipping he always takes with.

They make themselves known after every tragedy. Serial survivors. People who find themselves on exploding buses but never seem to die.

"Augurs," I say. "Harbingers of doom. They are demons. Dybbuks. We should march to their houses. Drag them to the squares and burn them in front of cheering crowds."

"You are stupid with nerves," Inbar says. "They are the

unluckiest lucky people in the world. These are hopeful stories from hopeless times. Without them the grief of this nation would tip it into the sea."

I'm swollen with heroism. The sad fact of it. Curled up on the bathroom floor woozy with the makings for a bold rescue, overdosed on my own life-or-death acumen. My body exorcises its charger of burning buildings, its icy-waters diver. The unused hero driven out while I wait patiently inside.

The chandelier, like a pendulum; the day, like a pendulum, swings.

Inbar will turn the corner in her apartment and find her American boyfriend pinned to the floor, immobile, sweating a malarial sweat.

She will discover him suffering the bystander's disease. She'll want to wrap him in a blanket, put him in a cab, and take him to the hospital where all the uninjured victims, the unhurt, uninvolved victims, trickle in for the empty beds, to be placed on the cots in the halls.

I do not want the hospital. Do not want treatment for having sat down after, for having sipped coffee after, and held on to the owner's hand.

A call home. Inbar dials the moment she thinks I can pull off a passable calm. My mother's secretary answers. Rita, who never says more than hello and "I'll get your mother." My phone calls precious because of the distance. As if I'm calling from the moon.

Today she is talking. Today Rita has something to share.

"Your mother is in her office crying. She don't say nothing to you, but that woman is miserable with you out in a war. Think about where you live, child. Think about your mom."

. . .

There is an element of struggle. Sex that night a matter of life and death. There is much scrambling for leverage and footing. Displays of body language that I've never known. We cling and dig in, as if striving for permanence, laboring for a union that won't come undone.

We laugh after. We cackle and roll around, reviewing technique and execution. Hysterical. Absurd. Perfect in its desperation. We make jokes at the expense of ourselves.

"No sex like near-death sex."

We light up a cigarette, naked, twisted up in the sheets. Again we would not recognize ourselves on TV.

Inbar has gone to work and invited Lynn over to make sure that I stay out of bed, that I go into town for coffee and sit at my café. Same time, same table, same cup, if I can manage it.

Nothing can be allowed to interrupt routine.

"Part of life here," Lynn says.

This is why Inbar invited her. She respects Lynn as an American with Israeli sensibilities. The hard-news photographer, moving in after every tragedy to shoot up what's left.

The peeper's peep, we call her. The voyeur's eye. Our Lynn, feeding the grumbling image-hungry bellies of America's commuter trains and breakfast nooks.

"A ghost," Lynn says. She is gloomy, but with a sportsman's muted excitement. "Peak invisibility. People moving right through me. I think I even went weightless at some point, pulled off impossible angles. Floated above the pack. My stuff is all over the wire this morning." She pops the top on a used film canister, tips its contents into her palm. "You've got to come out with me one day just for the experience. You can stand in the middle of a goddamn riot, people going down left and right. Arab kids tossing rocks, Molotov cocktails, Israelis firing back tear gas and rubber bullets. Chaos. And you move, you just slide right through it all like a fucking ghost, snatching up souls, freezing time. A boy in the air, his body arched, his face to the sky. He's lobbing back a gas canister, the smoke caught in a long snaking trail. Poetry. Yesterday, though. Yesterday was bad."

"I'm not made for this," I tell her. "I grew up in the suburbs. I own a hot-air popcorn popper. A selection of Mylec Air-Flo street-hockey sticks."

"Two of these," she says, and drops two orange capsules in my tea. "Drink up." And I do. "Two before I shoot and two right after I dump the film. An image comes back to haunt me, I take another. The trapdoor in my system. If it gets to be too much, I'll just stay asleep. So to show my utter thankfulness upon waking, I make a pass of the Old City the next day. I stop in every quarter, pray at every place of worship I find. That's my secret, a flittingness. I favor no gods. Establish again and again my lack of allegiance.

"That's what keeps me invisible. That's how I get to walk through the heart of a conflict, to watch everything, to see and see and see, then pack up my images and walk away. In return, nothing. A ghost. Sensed but not seen. That's the whole trick.

"Staying alive," she says, "means never blinking and never taking sides."

"I didn't look, didn't want the dreams. I went the long way around so not to see."

"Unimportant. Not how you see, but the distance that counts. The simple fact of exposure to death. Same principle as radiation or chemotherapy. Exposure to all that death is what keeps you alive."

"I feel old from this," I say.

"Good," she says. "World-weary is good, just what you

should be trying for. Go play the expatriate at your café. Go be the witty war-watching raconteur. Cock an eyebrow and have them spike your coffee. Ignore the weather and put on a big, heavy sweater. Pinch the waitress on her behind." ·

I was raised on tradition. Pictures of a hallowed Jerusalem nestled away like Eden. A Jerusalem so precious God spared it when He flooded the world.

I can guide you to the valley where David slew Goliath. Recite by heart the love songs written by Solomon, his son. There have been thirteen sieges and twenty downfalls. And I can lead you through the alleys of the Old City, tell you a story about each one.

This is my knowing. Dusty-book knowing. I thought I'd learned everything about Jerusalem, only to discover my information was very very old.

I move through town, down the street of empty windows and blackened walls. The cobblestones are polished. Even the branches and rooftops have been picked clean. Every spot where a corpse lay is marked by candles. Fifty here, a hundred there. Temporary markers before monuments to come.

I make my way into the café. I nod at the owner, look at all the people out to display for the cameras, for each other, an ability to pass an afternoon at ease.

I sit at my table and order coffee. The waitress goes off to her machine. Cradling my chin, I wrestle images: unhinged mouths and clouds of smoke. Blasts like wild birds.

Today is a day to find religion. To decide that one god is more right than another, to uncover in this sad reality a covenant—some promise of coming good. There are signs if one looks. If one is willing to turn again to his old knowing, to salt over shoulders, prayers before journeys, wrists bound with holy red thread.

Witchery and superstition.

Comforts.

A boom that pushes air, that bears down and sweeps the room. My hair goes loose at the roots.

The others talk and eat. One lone woman stares off, page of a magazine held midturn.

"Fighter," the waitress says, watching, smiling, leaning up against the bar.

She's world-weary. Wise. The air force, obviously. The sound barrier broken.

I want to smile back at her. In fact, I want to be her. I concentrate, taking deep breaths, studying her style. Noting: How to lean against a bar all full of knowing. Must master loud noises, sudden moves.

I reach for my coffee and rattle the cup, burn my fingers, pull my hand away.

The terrible shake trapped in my hands. Yesterday's sounds caught up in my head. I tap an ear, like a swimmer. A minor frequency problem, I'm sure. I've picked up on the congenital ringing in Jerusalem's ears.

The waitress deals with me in a waitress's way. She serves me a big round-headed muffin, poppy seeds trapped in the glaze. The on-the-house offer, a bartering of sorts. Here's a little kindness; now don't lose your mind.

Anchors. Symbols. The owner appears next to me, rubbing my arm. "Round foods are good for mourning," I say. "They symbolize eternity and the unbreakable cycles of life." I point with my free hand. "Cracks in the windows are good too. Each one means another demon has gone."

He smiles, as if to say, That's the spirit, and adds one of his own.

"A chip in your mug," he says. "In my family it means good things to come. And from the looks of my kitchen, this place will soon be overflowing with luck."

The waitress pushes the muffin toward me, as if I'd forgotten it was served.

But it's not a day for accepting kindness. Inbar has warned me, Stick with routine. Lynn has warned me, Don't blink your eyes.

And even this place has its own history of warnings. One set accompanying its every destruction and another tied to each rise. The balance that keeps the land from tipping. The traps that cost paradise and freedom, that turn second sons to firstborn. A litany of unburning bushes and smote rocks.

A legion of covenants sealed by food and by fire. Sacrifice after sacrifice. I free myself from the owner's hand and run through the biblical models.

Never take a bite out of curiosity.

Never trade your good name out of hunger.

And even if a public bombing strikes you in a private way, hide that from everyone lest you be called out to lead them.